Gunfighters & Ghostriders

Kaye Spencer

Lasterday Stories, LLC

Gunfighters & Ghostriders

1st Ed. Gunslingers & Ghostriders Copyright© 2006 Kaye Spencer (A.L. Debran)

2nd Ed. The Gunfighter's Woman Copyright© 2016 Kaye Spencer

3rd Ed. Gunfighters & Ghostriders Copyright© 2025 Kaye Spencer

Cover design – Livia Reasoner

Published by Lasterday Stories, LLC

www.lasterdaystories.com

All rights reserved.

ISBN: 979-8-9997445-7-9

Library of Congress Control Number: 2025917206

"Men's courses will foreshadow certain ends,
to which, if persevered in, they must lead," said Scrooge.
"But if the courses be departed from, the ends will change."

Charles Dickens

A Christmas Carol

Chapter One

Stirling Ranch east of Trinidad, Colorado

Early June 1890

It wasn't the first time her husband had returned since his death. A few weeks after his funeral, she'd awakened to find him standing at her bedside, a silent, oddly comforting presence, yet a disconcerting one all the same. Gregory had been as easy to talk to as he was a considerate listener, so she'd asked him why he was there. His voice came to her as a distant, hollow whisper on a breath as fleeting as butterfly wings in flight.

I'm watching over you until he arrives.

She knew well of whom he spoke. How often this mysterious man had come into her dreams, she couldn't say. She didn't know his name or his face, and he never spoke, but she knew his eyes—eyes as wild and untamed as the man himself. When he visited, he arrived from nowhere and left the same way, lingering just long enough in her sleeping mind for her to know he was waiting for her. There was strength and love in his heart, and she felt safe and satisfied whenever she dreamed of him. She couldn't explain why, but Gregory had felt it, too, for the man had wandered into Gregory's dreams not long before his death. He'd taken it as a portent of her future well-being and happiness, and because believing in this man gave him peace, Brenna accepted it, too.

On the first anniversary of Gregory's death, his chair near the fireplace began rocking of its own accord, and she'd realized his spirt was Earth-bound. In an effort to assist him in his spiritual journey, she moved out of their bedroom with the hope it would help him let go of her. While his nocturnal visits had stopped or, at least, hadn't followed her to the other bedroom, she still felt his occasional presence in other ways—the chair rocking, a whisper, a fleeting touch against her skin, a curtain fluttering in the absence of a breeze, the dogs lifting their heads as if watching someone she couldn't see cross the room.

And now, at Gregory's urging, Brenna Gérard rode out across the land where flash flood waters rushed off the northern slope of Johnson Mesa and down Trinchera Pass, filling the ancient dry creek beds with run-off that spilled across the thirsty plains toward the Purgatoire River.

Reining-in at her destination along Trinchera Creek, her buckskin gelding, Samson, dropped his head to graze, and Brenna inhaled the sweet, dusky promise of rain drifting on the breeze. Ominous, black roiling clouds building in the west reminded her it was unwise to be caught away from the protection of the ranch houses, but despite the shiver shimmying down her spine, she couldn't make herself turn back.

Kicking her feet out of the stirrups, Brenna rolled her shoulders against the ache in her back and pressed her fingers against her temples to ease the too-tired headache from all day in the sun. It had been a long, hard week of laying down flat rocks in what would eventually be foot paths between the houses and outbuildings inside the ranch compound. When she'd tamped down the last rock for the day and sifted sand between the cracks, she'd set her mind on chores, supper, bath, and bed, but she'd only managed to tend the livestock and clean up the supper dishes when Gregory had whispered, urging her to ride to the place along the creek where they used to picnic.

Samson shifted his weight and cocked an ear toward the low, rumbling thunder. Patting his shoulder, she said, "I hear it, fella. Just a few minutes more."

Turning in her seat, she looked back at the ranch compound spread out in the distance. This was her favorite view with the mesas and buttes cradling the buildings on three sides as if holding it within the protection of an Earthly embrace. Samson swished his tail and went back to munching grass. With a tired sigh, Brenna rubbed her hands over her face then tucked loose tendrils of her auburn hair behind her ears and lifted the long thick braid off her neck to let the cool breeze touch her skin.

A few fat raindrops plinked down as she gazed the length of the creek, seeing nothing but the thick mesh of bushes and trees and wondering again just what she was doing out here with the creek running high up the willows. On a deep sigh, she asked herself why she was so willing to acquiesce to Gregory's whispers. It was a silly question. She knew why. Theirs had been a love borne of respect and friendship, and it wasn't in her to dishonor that. So she waited.

When good sense to return home ahead of the storm overrode waiting, Brenna gathered her reins at the moment Samson's head came up with ears pricked and attention locked on something downstream. Shoving her feet into her stirrups, she leaned forward and glimpsed a dark blur of movement, then heard thrashing as if a large animal was fighting its way through the tangled mess of cedars and deadfall. Probably an elk or a deer. She tapped Samson with her heels, and he moved out with careful steps as he picked his way along an old game trail.

"Damn it to holy hell! *Shit!*" The man's words came on the crack of breaking branches and a loud splash.

A few cautious yards farther, she spied a mud-smeared horse standing wide-legged on the opposite bank. When the horse saw them, it swung its head up, nostrils flared and wall-eyed. In a glance, Brenna deduced the bank had caved in, taking horse and rider down the steep embankment and dumped them into the rushing water.

Dismounting, she dropped the reins and gave Samson a stay-put pat. She spotted the scar on the bank where the horse had gone into the water then clambered back out, but without getting perilously close to the unstable edge, she couldn't see the rider. For all she knew, he'd been swept away in the current. Taking easy steps, she tested the ground before putting her full weight down until she was close enough to see the man lying face down on the muddy bank, his lower body in the water, and one hand clutching a willow branch. Alive or dead, it didn't matter. She couldn't leave him there nor ride away with his horse stranded on the other side.

"You there. You in the water! Are you hurt? I can help you. Show me you're alive."

His horse peered down, ears forward and shifting his weight in an uneasy, nervous dance. Seconds ticked off.

"Mister! Wave or lift—"

The man rolled to his side, made a feeble wave, and fell back on his face.

Brenna assessed the situation. It wasn't that the creek was dangerously deep, even running this high, but right here the banks became narrow and steep. She saw no easy way to reach him, let alone bring him to her side and up the muddy bank to dry land. Lightning flashed with a rapid thundering response that brought a harder spattering of rain on a gust of frigid wind. No more dilly-dallying.

"I'm coming over."

Backtracking, she found a likely place a few yards upstream. Sitting on the edge of the bank, she dug in her heels to let herself down on a slow slide, but the bank gave way. Anticipating a cold dunking, she sucked in a deep breath just before she hit the water. Able to keep her feet and not go clear under, she used the current to carry her to the man.

Cold and breathing hard when she reached him, she grabbed his arm, and rolled him onto his back. "Can you move?" Lightning forked across the sky, and Brenna instinctively ducked at the expected crack of thunder. "We can't stay here."

The man opened unfocused eyes on a face plastered with mud and blood.

"Horse..." He groaned on shallow pants. "Horse... rolled on me. Hit—hit my head...my chest..."

"I can't help you here. We have to get to the other side." Putting an arm around his waist, she dragged him into the water with her. "Hold on to me. We're going with the current until we find a place to get out."

His weight and the water-logged leather duster he wore dragged them down like an anchor determined to take them to the bottom of the creek, but she managed to keep them both from drowning despite his cumbersome weight. Spying a likely place, she guided the man toward the bank. "Here. We'll climb out here."

With a firm grip on his coat, she dragged and hauled him up out of the creek. Brenna dropped beside him, resting her gloved hand on his heaving chest to steady herself while she caught her breath. Samson nudged her, and she rubbed his muzzle, not a bit surprised he'd followed along.

"We have to leave. Your horse is still on the other side. We can ride my horse to the ranch." She pointed to Samson and immediately felt silly for the gesture since the man's eyes were clamped shut in a grimace of teeth-gritted pain. Standing on shaking legs, Brenna leaned on Samson until she had her balance, then she tied the reins in a loose slipknot, and draped them over his neck.

Lightning slashed the sky with an explosion of thunder that shook air and Earth and deafened ears. The man came off the ground in a lunge, feet planted wide, and his attention fixed on the black billowing cloudbank rolling along McBride Mesa to the west. Mesmerized, Brenna stared at the clouds as they transformed into a mighty herd of cattle stampeding along the mesa's rim. As she watched, the herd curved east, dipping low along the ancient stone wall and then soaring into the sky. The herd doubled-back with the sinuous motion of a Chinese dragon in an undulating journey from ground to towering clouds and back down again.

On the second pass, the cloud-herd swung south and swooped down from Trinchera Pass, passing overhead on a blast of scorching wind. Brenna flinched and ducked as the lead steers overtook them. Samson snorted, bolted, but she held fast to his reins. Eyes blazing with the fires of Hell, the herd pounded the air with steely hooves on peal after peal of thunder as it swung out north across the prairie to come charging low over Pine Canyon on the east.

Then, the clouds split open into a sandy ravine that cut a wide, ragged path to a range in the heavens. Brenna felt their breath in a whoosh of hot wind and saw their black horns glistening and brands flaming with each lightning blaze as the ghost herd plowed up that draw.

"*No!* Not going. They're not taking me!"

"What *is* that?"

The man snaked an arm around Brenna's waist and tossed her to the saddle then swung up behind her. "Hang on!" Clamping one arm around her middle, he grabbed the saddle horn with his other hand, and slapped spurs to Samson.

The horse reared, leaped, and came down at a dead run, ears flattened against his head, and his neck stretched out. A mournful, skin-prickling cry cut through the air. Hot wind whipped their clothes; lightning-scorched air left an acrid Sulphur stench in its wake. Brenna twisted to look behind. The sight coming at them was terrifying and fascinating. Hurdling from the midst of the churning maelstrom of boiling black clouds came spectral cowboys riding hard and fast after the phantom herd on hollow-eyed, fire-snorting skeleton horses pawing the air as they roared toward them. A low keening wail rose on the wind.

Matthewwwww Matthewwwww Caddockkkkkkk.

The man warned, "Close your eyes! Don't look!"

But Brenna couldn't look away from the spectral cowboys charging over them, their gaunt eyes staring from fire-flaming faces as they swung around and away in their relentless pursuit of the ghost herd. Rain burst from the clouds; hail peppered down. A blast of frigid wind hit them broadside, bringing the eerie sound of a shrill whinny as the man's horse bounded up and out of the creek. The man grabbed a tighter hold around her, and she held onto the saddle pommel with both hands to keep her seat.

The man let Samson have his head, and they raced across the prairie and through the open gates of the ranch compound at full tilt. Worried about the man's horse, Brenna glanced behind to see him, stirrups and saddle fenders flapping wildly in his frenzied run to stay with them. Samson slid to a stop on his haunches, and the man threw a leg over the horse's rump. His legs gave out and he crumpled in a heap. Brenna bailed off and dropped to her knees beside him.

"Get up. We have to go in inside."

Brenna draped one of his arms across her shoulders, and they stood as one person. Staggering under his weight, Brenna dragged him, stumbling, the few feet to the porch and into the kitchen. She dumped him onto a kitchen chair, and though his right hand dropped to the gun and holster at his hip, his head lolled back as he teetered off the seat.

"*No no no no.*" Brenna righted him and scooted the chair to prop him against the table.

"Water. Need water," he croaked on a raspy whisper as his body slumped even farther.

"Of course. Right here." Brenna filled a glass from the pitcher on the cabinet counter. He grabbed the glass out of her hands and gulped, then grunted for more. She refilled and this time, he drank with less desperation, which afforded her a moment or two to look him over.

Raw skin peeked-out from the rips in his trousers. Blood seeped into his scruffy beard from the deep, angry graze along his left cheekbone. His hands, swollen and discolored with a motley mixture of colorful bruises and scabbed-over knuckles combined with the tell-tale signs of bruising on his cheeks, made her wonder if he'd come out on the losing end of a brawl. Dark, wet and muddy hair hung low on his collar, and shaggy curls stuck to the egg-sized knot on his forehead. His eyes didn't look quite right, and compounded with his shaky balance, gave her some concern for how hard he'd hit his head. Although, he was in no danger of succumbing to his visible wounds, she'd patched-up enough cowboys to suspect he'd taken a merciless beating before his horse fell on him.

The man emptied the glass, and his head nodded forward. The glass slipped from his hand, but Brenna saved it while managing to keep him from sliding off the chair.

"Here, now. None of that."

The man came back to his senses and sat up straighter, his breathing shallow, his face contorted against his pain.

"I need to tend your injuries and get you cleaned up. A good long rest wouldn't do you any harm, either."

He was no help as she peeled off his duster, then unbuttoned his shirt and drew the tattered garment over his shoulders and down his arms. A quick inspection revealed a bullet graze hardly more than a deep, seeping scratch along his ribs, and the point of his shoulder bore a fresh abrasion. His chest, upper arms, and back showed extensive bruising, which confirmed her belief someone had worked him over within the past few days.

His trousers and boots needed to come off in order to finish her examination, but getting him to his feet and keeping him upright while she checked him over wasn't likely to happen in his current state of fatigue.

"All right, cowboy, let's get you to a bed before you pass out. Stand up and put your arm over my shoulder." It took some doing to guide him to the nearest bedroom and maneuver him to the bed. With a steadying hand on the small of his back, she extricated herself from under his draped arm. "Here we are. I'll help you take off the rest of your clothes before you—"

His legs folded, and there was nothing she could do but go down with him. "Not on Grandmother's quilt!"

His weight, like that of a dead man's, pinned her beneath him, pressing her into the mattress with his face resting against her breasts, and his breath warm and moist against her skin. Her task at hand flew out the window with the feel of this stranger's hard, lean body holding her to the bed.

"Got. To. Lay...lay down. Clean my wounds. Need sleep," he muttered against her chest.

"Yes, I know." Brenna pushed him over and off while wiggling from under him. "That's what I'm trying to accomplish."

She'd just as well have been talking to a fence post. He was out cold with one dirty trouser leg on the mattress and the other hanging over the edge of the mattress. Flustered, she shook her head and clucked her tongue. He was a soggy, muddy mess. This was going to be a lot of work cleaning him up and changing the bed covers without including the extra laundry he'd created and the puddle his duster was undoubtedly leaving on the kitchen floor.

She mumbled, more in exasperation than resentment, "When you wake up, I hope you appreciate this."

Removing the pillows to keep them clean, she left him to build a small fire in the cook stove onto which she put a pot of water on to boil. Then, she went outside to the horses where they waited at the porch, heads hanging and tails tucked against drizzle that had set in.

Leading them to the barn, she put them into stalls that opened into the corral where they could get water, unsaddled and rubbed them down, then poured a small amount of grain into feed tubs and forked hay into their mangers. She checked the man's horse over, found nothing worse than scraped shins and hocks, then grabbed-up his gear and returned to the house.

She half-expected to see the wild phantom herd and the gaunt-faced cowboys hovering above the butte, but all that remained were the low, heavy clouds with steady, gentle rain, and distant grumbling thunder.

Back inside, she changed into dry clothes, then went to the man's room and lit the kerosene lamp. He hadn't moved. It took two trips to the kitchen to bring in the items she needed—kettle of hot water, bar of soap and a cloth in a dishpan, towels, and the medicine kit.

She pulled off his boots, tossed his worn-out-in-the-heels socks aside, then untied the strings around his thighs and unbuckled his gun belt, which then took some doing to work it out from under him. Lifting his dangling leg to the bed, she stretched him out so she could sit next to him.

"Looks like you fancy yourself a gunfighter. Outlaw, more likely," she muttered.

Proceeding with the businesslike detachment of a nurse, she undid his trousers buttons, grabbed the waistband with both hands, and went about tugging them over his hips. Another tug and the trousers came to his knees—and she stopped.

He wore not a stitch of underclothing.

Averting her eyes, she felt heat rising up her neck, and her cool detachment vanished. Reproving herself, she said, "What's wrong with you? You've seen naked men before." Blowing out a sharp breath between her teeth, she answered, "But not one this...attractive."

Out of modesty, once she finished her task of removing his soiled clothes, she draped a towel over his midsection. Then, thirty minutes later, she was satisfied his injuries were tended, and he was as clean and comfortable in the fresh linens as she could make him. She returned the bathing and medical supplies to the kitchen then went back to clean up the mess.

Lingering at his side, she allowed herself the luxury of admiring him. His face, angular with high cheekbones and a strong jaw was even more handsome with the shave and his unruly locks trimmed. The muscles in his arms and torso were well-defined and the skin browned from the sun, which indicated he was a man who knew how to do more with his hands than use a gun. He shifted position on a deep groan and kicked a leg from under the sheet, which pulled the covers tantalizingly low on his belly.

Grasping the sheet to draw it up, she let her fingers trail against his skin. Her mouth went dry; she licked her lips. The urge to throw back the sheet and gaze upon his nakedness with shameless appreciation was strong, especially when she closed her eyes for a moment to bring up the feel of his body pressing hers to the bed and his breath caressing her skin. Her body warmed with remembered passion of lying with a man, and for a few delicious moments, she allowed herself the fantasy of someday knowing that passion again.

Drawing the sheet to his chest, she lifted his leg back onto the bed, then took out a Whitney blanket from the cedar chest, and shook it out over him. Drifters often stopped in for a meal or water and to have injuries tended and broken bones mended. Some traded for fresh horses, but not a single one had turned her head.

But this man...

Dousing the lamp, she left the door ajar on her way so she could hear him if he called.

Chapter Two

Matt Caddock opened his eyes to a bleary world, vaguely aware he was lying on a soft bed, which was something that hadn't come his way more than a handful of times since— Well, since he couldn't remember when. What felt and smelled like an early morning breeze fluttered the curtains, and his foggy mind worked to place the unfamiliar surroundings. Barking dogs and a rooster crowing added to his confusion. For a second, he wondered if he was dead and in heaven, which was wishful thinking considering the reckless violence of his past. Still, curtains, a soft mattress, and chickens didn't seem like the right fittings for Hell, but on the other hand, there damn sure was a big three-headed dog guarding the gate to the Underworld, and those barking dogs didn't sound like yapping little lap-sitters.

When blinking didn't clear his vision, he rubbed his eyes and found a goose-egg-sized knot on his forehead. With a ginger touch, he explored his face to discover a cut along his cheekbone, split lips, and a sore jaw to go along with the bump and his nearly swollen-shut right eye. There wasn't a place on his body that didn't hurt, but the worst pain was in his hands. He held them up, squinting to focus uncooperative eyes—

Guns! Where're my guns?

He bolted up, craning to see everywhere all at once. His sudden movement brought forth a teeth-clenched growling groan of cursing at the pain burning from his shoulders down to his feet. When it let up, he scanned the room from framed wall hangings to the man's robe on the bedpost to the kerosene lamp and pitcher of water on the little table beside him. Rising on an elbow with slow, deliberate care, he caught a whiff of leather oil and tilted his head back to see his gun belt draped around the bedpost. Stretching, he managed to pull one of his old, but trusty Peacemakers from the holster and held it with thick, swollen fingers. *Cleaned and loaded.* No doubt the other had received the same care. Somewhat more at ease, he returned the gun to the holster, then got his hands around the pitcher and drank his fill.

Lying back on the pillows, he stared at the ceiling, flexing his fingers to loosen the stiff joints while he tried to make sense of the confusion in his head. Where the hell was he? How did he get here? What happened? Thinking made his head ache as much as bending his fingers made his hands hurt, so he gave up both endeavors and closed his eyes. Once the questions racing around his head slowed to a walk, he became aware of a scent he hadn't encountered since childhood—a sweet, flowery fragrance. Bringing the sheet and blanket to his face, he inhaled. Definitely a woman-smell, but not of perfume, more like a fresh, clean, sundried scent.

Woman... There'd been a woman. Before he could ignite that spark of memory, the mixed aromas of brewing coffee and baking bread made their way to his nose, and his stomach responded. He had no idea when he'd eaten last. Along with the aromas came the soft sound of a woman singing. He lay still, listening to the clang and clatter of kitchen noises and the waxing and waning of her voice as she moved about. He wished the door was opened wider so he could see her. His mother used to sing like that when she cooked.

It had been a long time since he'd slept on a real mattress, let alone on a bed with clean sheets, and it brought a smile. Pulling the sheet and blanket to his face again, he glimpsed his body under the covers.

Well, I'll be damned. Buck naked.

He looked toward the door, his aches, bruises, and sore chest forgotten at the thought of a woman undressing him. Grinning, he closed his eyes, and surrendered to the comfort of his surroundings. Curtains, clean linens, and naked in a woman's house. A man could do worse. The soothing woman-noises from beyond the bedroom door reminded him of the home he'd always wanted, but had forfeited years ago, and he slept.

***

Movement jostled Matt toward awareness, but he was trapped in a disoriented waking sleep, and he couldn't shake off the terror of dragging along the edge of a river, one boot hung-up in the stirrup of a runaway horse, while cattle stampeded out of churning black thunderclouds hell-bent to trample him to death. The nightmare cattle thundered on past him when the chain-springs beneath the feather mattress protested as someone sat near his feet. The blanket and sheet lifted and cool air touched his body from thighs to feet then soft, strong hands rubbed an ointment that warmed his skin.

Chancing a peek between slitted eyelids, he saw a woman's head, her auburn hair in a long lose plait that fell over one shoulder, moving to and fro with her rhythmic massaging movements. She hummed, completely absorbed in her task. He almost smiled when he recognized her song. He couldn't imagine he was much of a beautiful dreamer for the swelling he'd felt in his face and all the bruises, abrasions, and overall beaten-up places he'd seen on his body.

Not wanting to interrupt her, he concentrated on remaining immobile, but when her hand dipped between his thighs with her rubbing, a rush of interest perked-up where it had no business perking, given the circumstances. A couple more dips and that interest began stirring into a fast track to embarrassment.

He reached the point of too much to handle at the moment the woman drew the sheet over his legs and repositioned herself higher up his side. A cool, damp cloth with the faint tang of witch hazel dabbed his face. A glass bottle clinked on the bedside table, and he smelled a stronger medicinal odor with her gentle fingers rubbing salve into the raw places on his face. The mattress springs creaked, and he felt the warmth and pressure of her body leaning against his chest as she reached across to grasp his left hand. She smelled a lot like the sheets—fresh and clean with a hint of something sweet.

Her hands were strong and her touch tender as she worked the healing salve into his battered hands, bending and flexing the joints. When he thought she was finished, she picked up the other hand and continued the treatment. There had been few enough times in his life that a woman looked twice at him, and fewer times that he'd felt a woman's touch—never one as sensuous and inviting as hers. Much as he liked what she was doing, it was time to take control before he lost control.

He closed his fingers around hers, and she stopped humming. He thought she was holding her breath. With his free hand, he traced the back of hers, stroking his fingers up and down the length. Then, he spread his fingers in an invitation to see if she'd accept. He didn't know what possessed him to do that, but it seemed a natural thing to do. Seconds passed, then she entwined her fingers with his. He hoped this was the woman who had rescued him, and he hoped she wasn't married to a gun-toting husband for the way she was holding his hand.

"How long have you been awake?"

Her voice, deep for a woman's, flowed over him with a soothing cadence that was every bit as soft as her touch. She withdrew her hand, but remained at his side. The warm pressure of her hip cradled into the curve of his side reminded him again how long it had been since he'd been this close to a woman, and he treasured the feeling for the rare gift it was.

When he opened his eyes, his first sight of the woman was a memory he'd take with him to his grave. Her eyes, as blue as a dawning sky when sunrise chases the night into daylight, held a hint of vexation mixed with curiosity. The splash of freckles over her nose and cheeks stood out against her creamy-colored skin, which gave her an energetic, girlish appearance. But the man in him noticed right off the way she filled-out her blouse left no doubt she was all woman.

"Ever since you started rubbing that ointment on my legs. Roused me out of a bad dream, and then it started to make sense in my head about how I ended up here." He attempted a grin, but it hurt to move his mouth. "Truth be told, I was awake when you made coffee, but you sang me back to sleep. That coffee and baking bread smelled mighty good. How long ago was that?"

She busied herself with wiping excess salve from her hands. "This morning. You slept all last night, and it won't be long until dark. I wouldn't have given much for you when I found you last evening. You were a miserable sight, but you cleaned up pretty well. I may have gotten carried away in my ministrations. I hope you don't mind."

"I don't mind. I'm sure it's an improvement over what you started with." Pushing up on an elbow brought a grimace and a groan.

"Let me help you." Brenna fluffed the pillows, then helped him scoot up and rest his shoulders against the headboard.

"Thanks." Reaching for the bed sheet, he drew it up and noticed Brenna's gaze lingering on his belly where the top of the sheet rested. "Looking for something in particular?" He grinned despite the pain it brought on.

Caught ogling, a blush rose up her neck and reddened her cheeks, which made her freckles stand out even more. Damn, but she was a fine-looking woman. Lord, what was he thinking? He didn't even know her name. He'd not had much experience with women, decent or otherwise.

With a toss of her head, which sent her long braid flopping over her shoulder, she defended herself. "No." Hastily, she left the bed to fiddle with organizing the medicinal supplies in the basket. Then she cut him a sidelong look with a smirk and a teasing gleam in her eyes. "Do you have something you want me to notice?"

Much as he'd liked having her beside him, he was relieved in a sense of decency sort of way that she'd moved away. Chuckling, he said, "No. We'd best find something else to talk about."

"I think that is a good idea. What would you like to talk about?"

"Well, I recall you hauled my sorry carcass out of the creek, and we rode a mad race ahead of a storm."

"I have questions about that storm. There was an eerie specter, malevolence in it."

"Yeah. It was a fearsome sight." That was putting it mildly. He'd hoped never to see that herd and those ghost cowboys again. "I want to thank you for helping me. For getting me here. It couldn't have been easy. Probably saved my life."

"You're welcome."

"What were you doing out there?"

She hesitated then offered an offhanded shrug. "I often ride in the evenings when it's cool."

She was hedging, and he also knew not to cross any lines given his stranger status, so he changed the subject. "Did my horse happen to show up, and where am I?"

"Yes. He's in the corral, and I cleaned your saddle. It's in the tack room. As for where you are, you're in my house on my family's

ranch. It's the Rocking Bell S. My name is Brenna Gérard. Feel free
to call me Brenna."

He nodded. "The Stirling Ranch. I've heard of it. You're the ones
who built the compound back in the thirties as a civilian stockade
for several families, and then the army used it as a fort for a while and,
as I recall, it was a stage stop after that. I'd heard it said this place was
abandoned years ago."

"It was never completely abandoned, although it has fallen into
disrepair from a lack of adequate upkeep, which was a result of my
family's financial status until recently. It hasn't been a stage station
since the line moved north, but a couple of times a year, a stage will
come in for water or to wait-out a snowstorm. We don't keep a relief
team, though."

"This must be close to where Goodnight and Loving drove cattle
down Trinchera Pass for the water and to avoid the toll over Raton
Pass."

"Yes, it is. Many an injured or hungry stranger has found sanctuary and assistance here, as have travelers in need of food and shelter.
And we've buried a few, as well. Now, speaking of strangers, do you
have a name?"

He was tempted to give her an alias, but his instinct cautioned him
that this woman didn't take kindly to lies. "Matt Caddock." He met
her steady gaze head-on knowing full well he'd likely worn out what
little welcome he'd gained with that confession.

Chapter Three

"Well, Mr. Caddock, you're welcomed to stay—at least, until your hands heal. Gunfighters aren't much use to anyone when their hands don't work. Particularly one-eyed gunmen."

Despite the twinkling amusement in her eyes, he couldn't read where he really stood. "You've heard of me."

"Yes. You're a legend around here for the way you single-handedly blocked a stagecoach robbery and shooting at the Clifton House stop. You were riding as shotgun messenger and saved everyone without firing a shot. Your reputation was enough to back down the robbers."

He couldn't tell if she was impressed or making judgment. "Stories always get better with each telling."

"True, but I heard it first-hand from my Uncle Pete who was a passenger on that stage. Pete said you put yourself between the robbers and the two women traveling with young children. Pete had heard about your pearl-handled Peacemakers and the way you wore them, so he recognized who you were, and the outlaws apparently did, too. They rode away empty-handed without a shot being fired on either side." She looked him over with assessing scrutiny. "Pete said for no older than you were, you had the look of a man who had stared Death straight in the eye and backed him down."

Matt blew out a hard, slow breath. It was time to go. He'd worked himself into a corner, and he knew what was coming next. She'd start preaching about the road to hell being paved with good intentions, which would lead into the sermon of changing his no-account, sinful ways before it was too late. Unfortunately, the only clothes he saw were folded in a neat stack on a chair across the room, and they weren't his, and he wasn't desperate enough to leave here wearing that robe she'd laid out for him.

"I've handled what's come my way. No more, no less." It wasn't much of a defense, but it was all he had.

"I'm curious. Did you earn your moniker as the Cimarron Gunfighter from a talent you demonstrated somewhere down in the Cimarron country, or because it means wild and unbroken, like a mustang?"

"Take your pick." The words came out on a cynical tone that he hadn't meant, but it was too late to take them back. Out of habit when a situation became tense, he rolled his shoulders and flexed his fingers in preparation of the coming confrontation. "It seems all of a sudden that you're uncomfortable with me being here, and I'm needing some breathing room." Damn her blues eyes and form-fitting blouse. "So, ma'am, if I could just have my clothes? It's time for me to be moving on."

"You're wrong, Mr. Caddock. I'm not a bit uncomfortable. I believe the stories I've heard about you are grossly exaggerated."

"How's that?"

Her eyes sparkled with mischief. "How tough can you be? You not only allowed me to remove all of your clothing, you apparently have no recollection of other liberties I may have taken."

That set him back. He hadn't expected such a bold comment from a woman who seemed so reserved and proper. She intrigued him with her light-hearted manner and quick tongue. He'd not had many opportunities to talk with women, but the few he had spent a little time with seemed to like him, although he'd never had this much personal attention from a woman.

"Well, you're right on both counts."

She gestured toward the bureau. "Your clothes were not worth salvaging, so I've put out a fresh set for you. I'll have supper ready in a few minutes." Picking up the medicine kit and the basket, and with a glance over her shoulder as she went to the door, she said, "That door across the room opens to the area between buildings, and the necessary is on back, if you have needs of a personal nature." She left the bedroom door partway open behind her.

"Brenna," he yelled.

"Yes?"

"Call me Matt."

Tossing back the bedcovers, he swung his feet to the floor. It took another minute before he felt steady enough to stand, and stretching clear to his full height took even more time. He hobbled across the room to the chair beside his gear, bedroll, and rifle she'd stowed in the corner, all clean and tidy. His boots, dry and oiled, were the only part of his outfit he recognized. Shaking out the shirt, his reflection in the cheval mirror stopped him. Turning to face it full-on, the first thing he noticed was she'd trimmed his hair and shaved his beard, leaving a mustache that curved down around the corners of his mouth. He ran his fingers over the mustache, nodding approval. She was right. He did clean-up pretty good.

Moving his inspection on down his body, he poked and prodded at his menagerie of cuts, abrasions, and the mass of bruises that ranged from new-purple to older yellow-green. He couldn't decide which was worse—his horse rolling on him down the creek bank or the beating he'd taken. What he did know was he looked like hell warmed over, and he felt like it, too. Any which way he turned this around in his head, it all came out the same. What little luck he'd been granted in his life had somehow brought Brenna to him just at the right time, and he was grateful for that.

The clothes fit well enough, and socks without holes felt good on his feet when he stomped into his boots. Slinging his gun belt around his hips, he buckled and tied the rawhide strings, then looked around for his hat and was dismayed it wasn't there. It was new enough he'd not had time to break it in good and proper. His searching brought him back to the framed tintype of a man propped on the dresser top. Upon closer study, he wondered if it was her husband. He made another check of the room. There wasn't much of a woman's touch here, but there wasn't a lack of it, either. If the man wasn't her husband, maybe it was her brother.

But what did it matter? Even if she wasn't married, she'd not look twice at the likes of him. He was a drifting gunfighter, a man with a past, and only more violence in his future. What he felt was appreciation for her help, which was more hospitality than he'd encountered in most folks. He listened to Brenna's rustlings in the other room, enjoying these few rare moments of home. Then he caught himself. He'd best get those notions out of his head right then. Still, a man could dream, couldn't he? There was no harm in that.

Shaking off the feelings, he went outside to a late afternoon of dark clouds hanging low over the land and a mist in the air. After a few minutes, he returned and went to the kitchen. A few feet from the kitchen table, the root cellar door was open and propped against the wall, and Brenna stood with her back to him at a work table beside a counter top with hand pump and sink basin.

He'd been in houses with the same overall design of a joined kitchen and common area, a living room he'd heard it called, that merged into one big room. Two sofas, small tables, upholstered chairs, and a high-backed wooden rocking chair were arranged around a good-sized hearth rug laid out in front of a rocked fireplace with floor-to-ceiling bookshelves on either side. A variety of throw rugs lay scattered here and there upon the clean-swept cobbled sandstone floor.

"Please, make yourself comfortable." Brenna glanced over her shoulder.

"Thanks. The food smells good. My stomach thinks my throat's been cut."

There was her soft smile again, and it was easy to smile back.

"Mind if I take a look at your library?"

"Not at all."

He pulled a few books out, and though his eyes didn't focus enough to read, if he squinted just right, he could make out the titles in the bigger lettering. It seemed she had everything from Greek and Roman works to Shakespeare and Blackstone's volume on law and democracy and a book of poetry. He'd not had a lot of schooling, but reading had come easily for him, and with a natural yearning to learn, he read everything and anything he could get his hands on. His pa always said if a man applied himself and kept an open mind, he could get as good of an education by reading as he could attending a university. Matt believed it, too.

Leaving the books with some reluctance, but with hope he might stay around long enough to read a few, he took a slow stroll around the room, noting the furnishings and the overall construction. The walls, a combination of rock and sandstone, had been made for defense back in the days when the Stirling Compound had been a fort, and he recognized the rectangular openings in the walls as shooting portals. Although he doubted they were of much use now, he still nodded approval at the staggered placement for the wide field of vision and firing they offered and for the hinged covers that swung out or hooked closed against the natural elements. He assumed the closed doors off the living room were bedrooms or maybe a den and storage.

Cheesecloth stretched over windows to keep out insects, and heavy wooden shutters folded to the wall for protection from intruders, bullets, and the weather. The front door, a sturdy combination of wood and metal, held a shooting portal at a man's shoulder level. Right now, it was wide open and against the wall to let the breeze blow through the cheesecloth tacked to the porch door. He counted four dogs peering in with tongue-hanging, tail-wagging eagerness to be invited inside, and from the looks of the low-sided boxes stuffed with old blankets spread about the living room, each dog had a special place.

"If you don't mind me saying so, your dogs aren't much in the way of guard dogs. They didn't even notice when I went outside."

Brenna glanced toward the porch door. "We have no need for aggressive dogs. They're friendly to everyone. Mostly, they keep the varmints out of the yard and away from the chickens, and they bark when they see people coming up the road. I love them for their company."

What garnered his closest inspection was the arsenal of rifles and shotguns lined up on the wall rack by the front door and the shelves stacked with ammunition.

"This is quite a fortification against attack."

"Yes. It is. Each building in the compound is designed and out-fitted in a military fort fashion. The set-up has served to protect generations of my family and the soldiers who have fought here, although, we haven't needed to defend ourselves in many years. The weapons represent homage to a former way of life more than a necessity of survival nowadays." Brenna looked up from stirring the boiling pot on the stove. "The potatoes are nearly ready. Is there something you'd like while we wait?"

"Water would hit the spot."

"Pitcher's on the table. Glasses in the cupboard."

"Thanks." Matt pulled out at chair at the table and sat down with a full glass of water that he refilled twice. "Don't read anything into my question, but do you live here alone? This is a sizeable layout for one person to tend."

"No offense taken. Generally, this place is overrun with people and activity, but in March, Aunt Aggie and my brother Jim's fiancée, Dara Everett, left for Philadelphia to help with the preparations of moving the rest of the family here before winter sets in."

"You have a lot of family coming out?"

"No, just my parents and younger brother and sister. My mother's parents are native Philadelphians. My parents stayed back east until my sister finished her medical training, which she did this past spring."

"Doctor?"

"Yes. She is especially set on providing medical care to women and children."

"I can tell you miss them."

With a soft smile, Brenna said, "It's been so long since we've been together. Uncle Pete, Jim, and all of our cowboys are driving a herd of longhorns here from Texas. They started out west of San Antonio. I'm expecting them by the end of August or early September."

"I don't mean to argue, but it still sounds like you're here by yourself. It's unusual to find a woman by herself this far from a town or neighbors. Doesn't seem safe."

She faced him, her eyes dark and serious. "If you're wondering if I can take care of myself...yes, I can. Three drifters stopped in not long ago. They mistook my grandparents' hospitality as fear while assuming I was a mere helpless woman. One of the men neglected his manners, and his friends buried him at the insistence of my shotgun."

Matt sat back with his hands raised in truce. "Whoa. I get your point. I didn't mean to rile you."

"I'm not riled. I'm stating fact."

The stirring spoon she shook at him belied her words, and Matt worked hard not to smile.

"Neighbors stop by frequently to check on me, and there is a crew of mill riders that work for many of the ranchers in this area. They are millwrights from Germany. They keep the windmills working year-round. They pass through every so often.

"At the moment, yes, I'm alone, but only because Grandma Mary and Grandpa Charles left for Denver last week to spend some well-deserved time in the city and to purchase supplies, which they'll send ahead by rail to Trinidad and have freighted here upon their return." She turned back to the stove. "Are you asking because you're worried about your virtue?'

Matt grinned. "Well, you *did* take all my clothes off."

"Yes, I certainly did."

Although he heard smug satisfaction in her words, her smiling glance warmed him in a way that made him think she was glad he was here. He could get used to a place like this, and he could listen to her laughter all day long. Old and buried yearnings rose up, and he found himself thinking again about a home instead of the life he'd been living, which was looking down the next trail between his horse's ears. But there was caution there, too.

"You're a tease, and that could get a man in all sorts of trouble by misreading your intentions."

He wondered how she did that. How she'd gotten him to thinking in a settling down sort of way like it was something he could actually attain.

"Then I apologize. I should warn you that I have a bold, head-strong, say-what's-on-my-mind nature. At least, that's how my family describes me."

"I'd have to agree with them. I admire a woman who knows her mind and speaks it. I just don't want to end up looking at the shooting end of your shotgun with a one-way ticket to your cemetery like that other fellow."

As she drained water from the potatoes and transferred them to a serving bowl, she said, "Then be sure not to get drunk and try to break into my home. I warned him once. When he played sport of shooting at my dogs, I didn't warn him twice. His companions found digging a grave with the barrel of a shotgun as motivation to be quite an exhilarating experience."

Damn. The woman had pure steel running through her veins. "I'll keep that in mind, but, I was thinking more about not offending your husband."

"My husband?" She fumbled the bowl. "Why would you think that?"

"In the bedroom. There's a picture of a man, and you said your last name is Gérard, not Stirling, so I'm assuming you're married, although you don't wear a ring."

She glanced at her left hand, nodding. "Yes, of course. He *was* my husband, and that was our bedroom."

"Was?"

"He died a year ago last January."

"Oh. I'm sorry. It's got to be hard living here without him."

"Sometimes it is. He had been ill for a long time. It was somewhat of a blessing his suffering finally ended."

"Not to be disrespectful, and I don't mind, but am I wearing his clothes?" Matt looked down at his shirt, trying not to let his frown go full-blown.

On a light laugh, she said, "No. They're my brother's. He's nearer your build. My husband was much shorter than you and not nearly so—" Cringing on her words, her cheeks reddened.

"So...what?" he wondered just how bold she really was.

"Muscular." Although she was smiling, she didn't look at him as she removed a pan of biscuits from the oven while hastening on with a babbling explanation. "Normally, we do our summer baking and cooking at the outside hearth so as not to heat our houses. As long as we keep windows and doors closed during the day then open windows to catch the night breeze, the houses stay tolerably comfortable during the summer and autumn. But with the cool spell we've had this week, I've been cooking inside."

Matt let it go, amused at her flustered, inane rambling. He also liked that she'd embarrassed herself. It made him think she liked him just a little. Letting it lie, he asked, "What's this book here on the table?"

Brenna wiped her hands on a towel. "It's an 1872 edition of *Traditions, Superstitions and Folk-lore* by Charles Hardwick."

"You've got a ribbon marking a place."

"I was curious about what I witnessed yesterday, and I recalled reading about it in this book. Go ahead and open it."

"Best you read it to me." He pointed to his swollen eye. "I'm not seeing good enough to read much of anything."

Brenna sat across from him and opened the book. "'Wodin, mounted on his white or dappled grey steed, is known as the wild huntsman. He is recognized by his broad-brimmed hat, and his wide mantle. Whoever sees its approach must fall flat on the ground, or shelter himself under any odd number of boards, nine or eleven, otherwise he will be borne away through the air and set down hundreds of miles away from home, among people who speak a strange tongue. It is still more dangerous to look out of the window when Wodin is sweeping by. The rash man is struck dead, or at least gets a box on the ear that makes his head swell as big as a bucket, and leaves a fiery mark on his cheek.

"'He soars over forests and moor-sweeps with his legion of hell-hounds. Overhead the sky is covered with grey vapor, but a mist is on all the land; not a sound among the fir tops. A woodsman will hear a distant wail, a moan rolling through the interlacing branches that comes nearer and nearer. There is the winding of a long horn waxing louder and louder, the baying of hounds, the rattle of hoofs, and paws on the pine tree tops. A blast of wind rolls along. The firs bend as withes, and the woodcutter sees the wild huntsman and his rout reeling by in frantic haste.'"

She paused on a glance toward him. "There's more."

A cold knot replaced the hunger gnawing at his stomach. This was a story he knew firsthand. "Go on."

"'Sometimes it gallops through the stormy air as a herd of wild boars; but the spirits of which it consists generally appear in human form. The first token which the furious host gives of its approach is a low song that makes the hearer's flesh creep. The grass and the leaves of the forest wave and bow in the moonshine as often as the strain begins anew. Presently the sounds come nearer and nearer, and swell into the music of a thousand instruments. Then bursts the hurricane, and the oaks of the forest come crashing down. The spectral appearance often presents itself in the shape of a great black coach, on which sit hundreds of spirits singing a wonderfully sweet song. Before it goes a man, who loudly warns everybody to get out of the way. All who hear him must instantly drop down with their faces to the ground, as at the coming of the wild hunt, and hold fast by something, were it only a blade of grass; for the furious host has been known to force many a man into its coach.'"

Brenna turned the book around so he could see the illustrations. "This is what I saw—a form of the wild hunt."

Matt sat back, exhaling like it was his last breath, and shaking his head that he didn't want to comment.

"At the creek, you said, 'No. Not going. They're not taking me.' I think you've seen it before, because you warned me not to look back." She leaned forward, her arms crossed on the open book. "Matt, I heard them call your name. They were coming for you. Why?"

How could he explain that if she hadn't rescued him, he'd be riding with those cowboys right now, chasing that ghost herd, and his soul damned to hell for all eternity?

Chapter Four

Matt pushed back from the table. "Can we go outside and talk? I need some air."

Brenna untied her apron as she stood. "Certainly. Supper will keep. You can explain while I tend to chores."

"I don't mind helping. Many hands make easy work, as my pa used to say."

"Those are wise words. We embrace that philosophy in our family. While you're waiting on me, you should take a look at your gelding. He's skinned up a little, but nothing serious. I put salve on the scrapes to keep the flies off." Donning a light jacket, she asked, "Does he have a name? My buckskin is Samson."

"That's a good name for a horse. I call mine Socks." He shrugged, a little embarrassed.

"Socks fits him just fine." Brenna took up a sawed-off Remington 16 gauge shotgun from beside the door and dropped shells into her jacket pocket. Responding to his eyebrow raised question, she explained, "For snakes and miscreants. I can reload fast and under pressure."

"I'll remember that."

Brenna handed him a hat. "Here. You might find yours where you fell into the creek, but for now, you can borrow this one."

"Thanks." Wincing when the hat bumped the knot on his forehead, he cocked it at an angle then opened the porch door for Brenna to go out ahead of him. She grabbed the milk bucket by the wire bail, and they waded through a flurry of tail-wagging happiness and he took the time to pet each dog.

Walking beside Brenna, Matt looked around to get the lay of the ranch yard. The ten-foot-high rock wall created a rectangular perimeter blockade that met on the north at the double wooden gates, which were swung open to a prairie view. He saw a smokehouse and a carriage shed. His perusal lingered on the iron-working and blacksmith equipment under a two-walled shelter that blocked a northwest wind.

The front doors of outbuildings and houses faced the common courtyard at the center of which was a windmill that pumped water through a small pipe that emptied into deep and wide stone and mortar trough in a thin ebbing and flowing stream of clear water. Nestled in the midst of a small grove of trees a few yards from the windmill was a covered well with hand pump, and opposite that was the stone hearth. Under the shade of the trees stood a long wooden table with benches that looked big enough to seat two dozen people or more.

Flower beds of blooming colors, kitchen gardens, Rose of Sharon bushes, and a tree here and there all added a happy, bright look to the tans and browns of the compound. The flat-rock foot paths, some complete and some marked-out to finish, connected each building to its neighbor with what appeared to be plans for additional paths to fork out to the hub of windmill and well like spokes on a wheel. It was a rock-wood-adobe oasis on the prairie with a decent set-up for defense and minimal worry for a fire spreading.

Beyond another set of gates, he saw the barn, good-sized hay sheds, corral, and another windmill, and he commented on it. "Those look newer than the rest of the buildings."

"They are. There's not much need to keep livestock close any more. The threat of rustling is slight, and we have fewer flies buzzing around the houses with the animals farther out. And really, closing the gates at night is a ritual rather than a necessity." Brenna surveyed the area, her body turned partially from him. "Do you like what you see?"

He did like what he saw. She was a fine looking woman, but more than that, she was a woman who could handle herself without resorting to the feminine tricks he'd encountered with some women. But that's not what she meant, and he responded as she expected.

"I do. If you need to, it's easy to defend from the inside and hard to breach from the outside. It's good that you have wood stored in lean-tos. The water is in a protected location and accessible from all directions, but not so far away as to be a chore hauling a full bucket to the house. I noticed the sink pump in your kitchen right there with your worktable. It lessens the trips to the well, and you're not trapped inside without water."

"Yes, and we water the flowers and shrubbery with the soiled water we've used, instead of just throwing it out on the ground. It's taking time, but we're slowly improving the premises with the latest conveniences."

"Where do you get the rocks for the foot paths?"

Brenna gestured to the south. "At the base of the dike that runs along the foot of Johnson Mesa. I've used my stockpile, so it's time to make a few trips out with the buckboard."

Socks nickered, came up to the corral fence, and Matt ducked between the poles. He stroked the bay's wide, white blaze, and ran his hands over his white-stockinged legs to check the minor cuts and scrapes. Satisfied with Brenna's assessment of no serious damage, he patted the horse on the rump as he cast a quick glance toward McBride Mesa. A shiver prickled his neck hairs at the memory of that spectral sight.

"I find myself looking at it, too." Brenna drew her attention from the mesa and folded her arms on a corral pole. "Tell me about the wild herd and those cowboys."

With his back to the fence, just down a couple of feet from Brenna, he hooked a boot heel on the bottom pole, and rested an elbow on a rail.

"I've only seen it one other time. I'd heard stories since I was a kid, but I'd never known anyone who'd really seen it." Socks nudged him, and Matt ran his fingers through the horse's mane, idly untangling strands from the dried mud.

"Until?"

"It's a long story."

"I'd like to hear about it."

Her smile, as soft as her words, encouraged him to tell her about his life, the little there was to tell. "I was born down on the Cimarron. When my ma died, Pa couldn't stand staying there without her, so he joined up with a cavalry unit as a tracker and scout, and he took me with him. For a couple of years, this worked out for us. I learned about living off the land and tracking. I rode about every trail there was in the Texas Indian country, and my pa made a few trails of his own. We were with a small cavalry patrol when we got into a scrape with some Comanche and Kiowa down along the Red River."

Matt looked on past Johnson Mesa in his mind's eye to that scene. "Pa took a Comanche arrow to his chest and died right there beside me. I didn't know what else to do, so I grabbed up his rifle and commenced to shooting."

"How old were you?"

Her words brought him back from the memories of that terrible day. It wasn't something he liked to think about. He missed his pa and his mother every day of his life since they'd died.

"Thirteen."

"What happened to you then?"

Matt leaned a shoulder against the fence. "Henry Buckholt sort of adopted me. We'd taken a liking to each other some months before. He said I'd left the boy in me behind when I'd taken up my pa's rifle, but I wasn't ready to be turned loose on my own yet."

"He was a soldier?"

"No, old buffalo hunter. When he wasn't prospecting or driving stage, he worked for the army however they needed him. Scout, cook, hostler, gunsmith. He could do just about anything he put his mind to."

"Did you stay with the army?"

"No. We traveled. California to the Mississippi River and everywhere in between, north to south. We followed a trap line high up in the Rockies one winter. He worked as a swamper in a saloon one whole year so I could go to school and get better at reading and cyphering. When he was ready to move on, he bought some books and that's how we spent our nights—me reading to him. His schooling wasn't much, but he could read and write enough to get by. I read anything I could get my hands on, and I got a pretty good education that way."

"Where is Mr. Buckholt now?"

Exhaling hard, he said, "Henry died the summer I turned twenty-one." Tight hurt welled in his chest, and he dug the toe of one boot into the dirt, unable to look at her. Losing Henry felt the same as losing his parents, maybe even more.

"Matt, I'm so sorry. You've had much loss in your life."

When Brenna placed a gentle hand on his shoulder, Matt ducked his head to hide the unaccustomed mist that blurred his eyes. That hadn't happened in a long time. She seemed in no mind to move away and that simple gesture softened a little of the loneliness he carried with him. He wanted to put his hand over hers, but he was afraid she'd pull away, and he'd lose this special moment too soon.

"I can see he meant a lot to you. How did he die?"

He saw it in his memories as plain as if he were back on that Arizona desert stage road. "Back in seventy-eight when gold was discovered some fifty miles north of Tucson, Henry went to work on a stage line running out to the mining towns around Mammoth. I rode in the box with him as shotgun messenger. We'd been driving that route for a year or better and had built up a reputation for busting right through ambushes and the only time we'd been held up, not a single robber lived to tell about it. We were on the return run back to Tucson with mail, some gold, but no passengers, when a storm brewed up out of a clear blue sky.

"I'd noticed Henry looking pale, and he was sweating like he had a fever, but he maintained there was nothing wrong when I asked him. All of a sudden, he grabbed his chest and keeled over on me. I got the team stopped and Henry to the ground.

"He grabbed my shirt and pulled me down close to talk right in my ear. He was weak, and I couldn't understand what he was saying. Then he had a burst of strength. He sat up and pointed to that storm billowing up behind us, and he yelled, *They're comin' for me!*"

"Like the clouds we saw yesterday?"

"Just like yesterday." Matt cut a guarded glance toward the sky. "There I was down on my knees holding Henry in my arms with that storm bearing down on us. Henry started talking fast, and I could tell it pained him to even take a breath. He told me he'd seen the ghostriders one night on a mountain top, then again not long before I hooked up with him. He said he'd done some mighty mean things in his life and now his soul was bound to ride with those cowboys through all eternity, never able to catch that herd, just chasing them forever in payment for the sins committed in his life."

The words were etched in his mind as clear today as when Henry had uttered them.

Takin' care of you was the only unselfish thing I ever done in my life. If there's any atonement for me, it'll be because of you. Matt, I found gold a long time ago. It's yours now, but you'll have to do some lookin' to find where I hid it. Go back to the Lady of Guadalupe in Taos. She's keepin' watch over a letter I left for you. But you got to promise you'll leave the gold alone until you know you'll use it for somethin' decent, somethin' right. Find yourself a good woman and make that home you lost when your folks died. You got to promise me, Matt. Promise, so maybe someday in the hereafter my worthless soul will find peace, because I'm headed for Hell sure as shootin'. You got to promise me.

"I gave him my word that I'd leave the gold alone until I could do something good with it. He died there in my arms with a smile on his face. Lightning was striking all around, and that ghost herd thundered right down on us with their steely hooves pounding the air and red fire burning in their eyes with those cowboys calling his name on the wind. They took him. One second he was there, the next...gone. Not a trace left." He blew out a long, slow breath.

"Nothing? Just vanished?" Her words held the same skepticism as her raised eyebrow held questions. "How is that possible?"

Matt shrugged, understanding her doubt. "I've asked myself that same question, and I don't have an answer, but it happened, just the same. I piled some rocks up in a shallow wash-out, and tied up two pieces of deadfall in a cross as a marker. Then I heated up a piece of iron and burned his name with the date he died on it. I couldn't leave there without making some sort of remembrance for him."

"There's emptiness in your voice. Longing and, maybe, regret?"

"He sure enough left a big hole in my heart."

"What did you do with your life then?"

"I drove that stage on to the end of the line, took my pay, and just started riding with no destination in mind. Henry had some skill with a six-shooter, and I was an eager student, so I took advantage of that learning and honed it. It wasn't long before I left a man dead in a shootout in El Paso, and another dead in Santa Fé. I collected the bounties. It was the easiest way to make money I'd ever had. I was fast on the draw, and I already had a reputation as that Injun-fighting kid from the Cimarron. Riding shotgun messenger with Henry on his stage runs had gone a long ways toward garnering me some respect for as young as I was. There were times I hired on with some stage and freight companies to make sure the passengers and shipments made it to where they were going. Once, I went north with a cattle drive on the Chisolm Trail."

"What became of the gold?"

Chapter Five

"Never looked for it. Didn't have a reason. I'm pretty sure I wouldn't put it to good use if I had it. Mostly, I don't believe it exists—except in an old man's wishes of better days."

Brenna tugged Matt's shirt sleeve. "I want to hear more, but let's do chores before it gets any darker and supper gets any colder. You can tell me the rest of your story while we eat."

They went through the open double wagon doors to the dusky interior of the barn, but it was obvious from the efficient manner in which she went about tending the animals, she'd done this so often, she could do it in the dark. She forked hay into mangers then poured a small amount of grain into each of several buckets scattered about the corral and also into grain boxes in a stall in the barn.

On her way to the gate on the west side of the corral, she checked the water level in the long windmill trough that was positioned to provide water in both the corral and the pasture. Satisfied, she let in the dozen or more horses and two pack mules, her buckskin, along with two cows and calves that all waited eagerly on the pasture side of the corral fence. She spoke to and petted each animal as they went past her on their way to designated tubs of grain.

Cats of all sizes and colors rubbed their legs and swarmed around Brenna as she milked one of the cows right in the corral, then she poured a pan full of milk for the cats. The chicken house, which butted up against the outside of the barn opened into the barn itself and the hens and roosters had free roam. It had one access door with a chicken-sized opening at the bottom. Brenna stepped inside, counted heads, came up with the right number, then inserted the little slider door over the opening, and locked them in from night predators.

Matt observed all of this from a position where he could also study the two colts and the filly. They were good stock, stout and straight-legged with intelligent eyes. They didn't show saddle marks, so he figured they were just at the right age to break to ride. If he was looking for a real reason to stay, this was it.

"All done, and I'm hungry."

Matt closed the double doors and dropped the bar into place. "Me, too." Together, they drew the two overlapping wall gates into place that, when open, formed an alleyway to bring animals into the yard and, when closed, completed the stockade barricade.

With shotgun in one hand and milk pail in the other, Brenna headed for the house. Matt fell in beside her. "Let me carry the milk. I'd offer to carry your shotgun, but you might misconstrue my intentions."

Brenna laughed. "Yes, I might at that, but don't assume without my shotgun that I'm at a disadvantage to protect myself. There are weapons well-placed and not necessarily in plain sight all over this compound, including the barn. I am always armed. Just because I'm without my shotgun doesn't mean I'm ill-prepared."

Matt chuckled with her. "No, ma'am, I'd never assume you can't protect yourself." He cut a sidelong glance toward her and took his chance. "Now that I know how you do your chores, I'd like to stay around and help, maybe break that filly and those two colts to ride."

Where there had been lighthearted banter was now solemn quiet. The way she turned her face away and tilted her head made him think she was listening to another conversation, but that was a crazy notion since they were the only two people there. All he could figure was he'd spoken out of line, and she was too much of a lady to come right out and ask him to leave after just having offered him a place to stay while he recuperated. But when she didn't respond by the time they reached the porch, he was kicking himself for being a big-mouthed fool.

"I didn't mean anything by what I said." He winced and attempted an apology. "I just want to show you how beholden I am for helping me." When she still didn't respond, he took it for what it meant. "If you'd be more comfortable, I'll pack up my gear and get on down the road."

"No, no, not at all." Flipping her braid over her shoulder, Brenna turned to him with a forced smile. "I appreciate your gracious offer, but you owe me nothing. I'm glad to help you." She brushed past him.

Encouraged she wasn't sending him packing, but confused by her sudden cold shoulder, he caught up with her to open the kitchen door just as she grasped the handle. Closing his fingers around her hand, he held it, his chest pressed against her shoulder. He was too close, and he hadn't intended to touch her, but when she didn't pull her hand away, he took his second chance.

"You didn't say if I'm welcome to stay around for a while."

Seconds passed before she looked at him. Her eyes shone with something he'd never seen from a woman, and the crazy idea to kiss her pushed at him, but he caught himself. What the hell was he doing? He was a gunman with nothing to offer a woman. He had no right to be thinking what he was thinking about her.

Releasing her hand, he stepped back. "I'm sorry. I was out of line—"

"Please, don't apologize. Consider the bedroom yours, unless you'd be more comfortable in the bunkhouse." She made an offhanded wave toward the yard.

His pa hadn't raised a fool. "The bedroom is fine. I like the company here."

Without a look in his direction, Brenna went inside amid a swish of skirts that allowed two dogs to sneak in with her. Matt lingered in the doorway, watching, and wondering what had changed. She'd been talkative and friendly a few minutes ago, and now her invitation for him to stay didn't match her stiff back and squared shoulders. At a loss of what to say, he stood at the doorway, waiting for her to make the next move.

Speaking over her shoulder, Brenna said, "We'll have supper at the summer table under the trees. Come in and fill your plate and pour a cup of coffee. Cups are in the cupboard to the left."

"Thank you." Relieved she was talking again, even if it was mundane, Matt hung his hat on a hook beside the door and took the plate she held out.

"With the clouds breaking up, we might have the light of the coming full moon."

He took the hint from her neutral talk about cups and weather that she'd erected an invisible barricade between them, but for the life of him, he couldn't figure out why. But one thing he did know was to keep his mouth shut until she gave an indication of what was on her mind.

They sat across from each other with the dogs settled at their feet. As evening blanketed the land, night noises emerged out of the darkness—crickets singing and toads croaking near the windmills, coyotes yipping somewhere on the prairie.

The silence building between them gave Matt the feeling he'd best be moving on with first light, but just as he worked up the right way to say it, Brenna spoke.

"How did you end up at the creek?"

Matt put his fork down and took a swallow of coffee. "You sure you want to hear it? I'm not real proud of it."

"Yes. I'm quite intrigued with what you've experienced in your life."

"A couple of years ago in Waco, I fell in with a man by the name of Archer. We rode north into the Rockies, and got into a skirmish with a band of renegade warriors, and I took an arrow deep in my leg." He patted the outside of his left thigh. "Archer cut it out, but I got passing-out drunk to let him do it. Somewhere in my drunken haze, I talked about Henry and the gold, but I don't remember what I said.

"When I sobered up, Archer asked about it. I said there was nothing to it but my mouth running from the whiskey and the rambling wishes of an old man who'd died dirt poor. I told him Henry was out of his mind in those minutes before he died, and there wasn't any gold. For a while, Archer dropped it, but by-and-by, he made off-hand remarks that extra money would make his life a lot easier. Then he started prodding me about keeping secrets from my saddle partner."

"*This avarice strikes deeper, grows with more pernicious root.*"

Matt nodded. "Macbeth."

Brenna smiled. "Yes. I also read everything I can get my hands on."

Matt smiled back with the feeling that whatever had set her on edge was letting up. "And I'll bet you went to college."

"I did. Now, back to why you ended up in the creek."

"I split from Archer some months back and rode down into Texas, then swung up north. I stopped at Maxwell and there was Archer and some hard-cases he used to ride with. He asked if I'd gone after the gold, and I told him again it didn't exist. He didn't believe me any more than he had the other times. They jumped me just out of town, and took me to a shack up in the hills. Archer told his men if they could beat the location of the gold out of me, they could have a cut."

"That explains your bruises."

"Yeah, they put away a few bottles of whiskey while they worked me over. Just before I passed out, a big man they called Vernon stomped on my hands. That's the only reason they left my guns on me. They figured I couldn't use them." Matt chuckled. "But that's where they went wrong. I came to and made a leap off the floor with swollen fingers clamped around a gun butt and my other hand fanning the hammer. I put lead into a couple of them. Then, I kicked over the oil lamp, and it started the place on fire. I busted through a side window and ran around back where the horses were tied. Socks took me out of there at a dead run in a helluva rain."

"You could have gone any direction. Why did you go up on the mesa?"

Matt shrugged. "We'd been heading north when we stopped in Maxwell, so I guess Socks found a trail he liked going that way. I just hung on for the ride." Feeling more at ease the longer he talked and she listened, he knew without a doubt he liked where that trail had brought him. "I don't remember much except being cold and soaked to the bone." He reached down and scratched one of the dogs behind the ears.

"I recall riding in a steady drizzle—don't know how much time passed—and when we came down off that mesa, the creeks were deep and running too fast to ford. My thinking wasn't clear, and I must have ridden too close to the bank, because it gave out under us. I remember Socks rolling over me and something hit me upside the head. I must have blacked out. Somewhere in all that, I was flat on my face on a muddy creek bank with you calling to me."

"That's an incredible story. It's a wonder you're alive."

"I wouldn't be if you hadn't come along."

"Which brings us to why that ghost herd and those phantom cowboys were chasing you."

Matt toyed with his empty coffee cup. This was a little harder to explain, and he needed to think it through. "How about I take our plates inside and bring out the coffee pot?"

"All right."

When he returned, he put the pan of biscuits, jar of jam, and the coffee pot on the table. "Darn good biscuits. Thought I'd have a couple more."

"I'm glad you like them."

Matt ate a biscuit and chased it with a gulp of coffee. Brenna seemed content to wait for him to get his thoughts together. He couldn't pin down a logical place to begin, so he just started talking.

"In the years since Henry died, I've studied on what happened that day on that Arizona stagecoach road. Even though I don't have the gold, and I've never considered in a serious way of looking for it, the road I took after Henry died was a road paved with death and violence." He shook his head, shrugging that he couldn't put the right words to what he wanted to say. "Maybe my time was up...and those riders were coming for me."

"But you said Henry saw the riders twice before they took him on the third time. This was only the second time you've seen the ghost herd. Perhaps it was merely a warning to change your ways before it's too late."

Matt exhaled, nodding. "That's crossed my mind. Whatever the reason, I hope this is the last time they come looking for me."

"That is my hope, as well. It was frightful."

"Now, I've got two questions for you."

"Oh? And they are?"

"Earlier—when we were in the barn—you were generous with your smile and light in your conversation. But when I said I'd like to stay around and help out, I had the feeling you regretted not letting me drown in that creek."

Brenna's easy smile and soft laughter held an apology. "No, no regrets. I realized I'd overlooked something that was plain as day. I'm sorry if I offended you. I was distracted in my thoughts for a few minutes."

"That's not an explanation, but it's not unreasonable, either. Now, my second question is one I've already asked."

"Why was I riding that far from shelter with a storm brewing?"

Matt nodded. "Yeah. I want the real reason. I don't buy that it was coincidence that you just happened to be where I was stranded."

Seconds ticked off before she replied. "My husband, Gregory, told me to ride out there."

"Hold on." Matt sat up straight, his head cocked, and an eyebrow arched. "You said he died."

Brenna looked at him. "He did."

"Your dead husband talks to you?"

Chapter Six

Brenna ran her finger around the lip of her coffee cup. Matt would either believe her, or he wouldn't. There was no use soft-soaping the truth, crazy though it seemed to him and sounded to her.

"He doesn't actually speak aloud. It's more that I sense his words." Inwardly cringing at his coming reaction, she added, "His voice is a distant whisper that I hear in my head or a warm breath at my ear."

"Did he say something to you when we walked to the house just a while ago?"

"Yes."

"You were friendly one minute and not the next like you regretted inviting me to stay."

"I'm sorry if I offended you."

"You didn't, but I'm curious about what he said to you."

The skepticism in his voice and the suspicion that she was crazy as a loon showing on his face amused her. "He advised me to tell you the real reason you're here."

He nodded, considering her words, but the way he moved his mouth in not quite a grin or a frown told her he didn't believe her story. "I've never met anyone who admits they hear voices."

"My brother, Jim, is the only person who knows I have conversations with Gregory. He calls it my popinjay intuition. I know it's incredible, but considering we were pursued by a ghost herd being chased by phantom cowboys yesterday, my story is tame in comparison."

Matt rested his elbows on the table and leaned forward. She hadn't noticed until now that his smile was like a little boy's, a little lopsided and completely honest in its openness.

"Point taken. Thank Gregory for me that he sent you out looking for me."

"Are you mocking me?"

Matt shook his head, his expression less skeptical. "No. I can see there's something afoot here beyond our understanding. Whatever it was—or whoever—I can accept it for the turn of good luck it was and leave it at that. I've come across some strange sights in my travels that have no rational explanation."

"There's more." Brenna swallowed hard, but she didn't look away.

"As in you're going to tell me the real reason I'm here...like your husband told you to."

"Yes. You'll probably find it difficult to accept."

"I'll do my best to not make judgment."

A little whirlwind blew through the compound, rustling the canopy of leaves sheltering their table and turning the windmill blades a creaking half-revolution before it moved on out to the prairie beyond the compound walls. The calm night returned, and Brenna took a deep, fortifying breath that she blew out in a slow exhale and forged onward.

"I believe we were destined to meet." She paused to allow him time to ponder her words. "And to be together."

Matt dipped his chin as he drew out the question. "Together as in..."

It was too late to backtrack now. "Lovers. Perhaps married. I—I don't know."

Matt's mouth opened on a wordless response then snapped shut. He sat back and combed fingers through his hair with frown lines deepening across his forehead. "You're right. You do say what's on your mind. Just...just why do you think that?"

"The day I married Gregory, as we held hands and exchanged our vows, for a moment I saw another man's eyes reflected in his. Then as time passed, the man came to me in my dreams. A faceless man with dark eyes that seemed to look into my heart. I didn't admit this to Gregory until many months into our marriage and, even then, it wasn't until he mentioned having odd dreams about a man who would appear from nowhere, perhaps out of a fog or mist, and he would offer his hand to me, and I would take it.

"Gregory believed we only had to pay attention to the world around us to find omens of what was to come in our lives. He was convinced we shared mirror dreams, and that I would find this man after he was gone. In time, I believed it, too."

***

Anticipating Matt's arrival into her life had made him real in an ethereal sense in the same way that sitting an arm's length from him now made him real in a tangible way, and telling him her secret confirmed its truth in her heart. Matt poured more coffee and wrapped both hands around his cup. He didn't look up. She knew he needed time to think, so she held her tongue as long as she could.

"Please, say something, even if it's goodbye."

Nodding, but not looking at her, he said, "This is... This is... Hell, I don't know what it is."

"Inappropriate? Scandalous? Shocking?"

"Any of those will do." He fumbled for words. "We... We don't know each other. We haven't courted."

Brenna leaned forward. "Matt, I've known you in my head and in my heart for years. In the deepest part of myself, I knew I would end my days with you." She whispered what she'd yearned to know every night as she gazed out her bedroom window in those moments just before sleep. "Haven't you ever wished for me?"

Matt came around to her side of the table, and she swung her legs over the bench as she swiveled to face him. The moon's glow cast light on his eyes that were prayer serious.

"Well, I've never had a dream like yours, but thinking about a woman to settle down with has kept me company over a good many miles and for a good many years."

"Maybe you've been riding all over this land looking for me."

She took his hand when he offered, and he brought her up to her feet.

"Brenna, I'm a no-account gunfighter with nothing to show, or offer, except what I carry in my saddlebags."

"That's not important right now." Brenna put her fingertips against his lips. "Kiss me, Matt. Surely, there's no harm in a kiss."

Matt leaned into her, his breath warm against her cheek as he brushed his lips against her skin. Tilting her face up, she met his lips. He smelled of tobacco, coffee, and man. He slipped an arm around her waist, drew her closer, and she molded her body to his. For a few moments, she lost herself in his arms, in his kiss. The kiss she'd imagined.

Matt rested his cheek against her hair. "Wishing for that kiss put me to sleep on many a cold, lonely night."

"As it did for me," she whispered.

"What happens now?"

"I don't know. I only know how our story begins."

Matt stepped back. "We've got to think this through."

"Yes, we do. Daylight changes what the night brings about, and sleep clears the mind of doubts. Shall we go back to the house?"

"That sounds like a good idea."

Once inside, Matt struck a match and touched it to the wicks of two oil lamps while Brenna put the dirty dishes into a wash basin and poured hot water from the pot she'd left warming on the stove top over them.

"Brenna."

She faced him. The anticipation of goodbye stung her eyes, but she held it back with stern determination to accept it graciously.

"Until ten minutes ago, I was a drifter headed down the next trail and looking for the next gunfight. I've got a few dollars in my pocket, but not enough to brag about. When I woke up this afternoon and saw those pretty blue eyes of yours, I had a powerful wish to stay here. You talked about the cattle coming in and your family on their way, and when I looked this place over, I felt I could stay here and never wonder again what man waited for me with intent to outdraw me just because of the challenge to beat me.

"It's a strong temptation to believe what you've told me, but I can't honestly say I'd be accepting your invitation with the right intentions. I'm tired and beaten up, and I need a place to rest for a while. Any place but where I've been is mighty inviting."

Brenna wiped her hands. "I understand." She hoped the disappointment in her heart didn't come across in her words.

Matt shook his head. "No, I don't think you do. What I'm trying to say is I'm trouble. Trouble with a temper and twelve ways of dying tied to my legs. I sell my guns, and I kill men for the price on their heads. I draw my guns at the slightest trouble, and I don't care who dies so long as it isn't me. I never walk away from a fight, and more times than not, I go looking for one. Brenna, I gave up my chance for a decent life years ago."

"What you've done in your past doesn't have to define the choices you make in the future."

Matt crossed the space between them. "In the last few minutes, I've relived my entire life in my head. I saw my gunfights. I rode back down all the trails of the men I hunted for the bounties. I counted the blood money I took without caring whose side of the fight was right or wrong. I held Henry in my arms as he died. I saw those ghost cowboys coming for me yesterday—" He blew out a hard breath on a harder sigh.

"All I ask is that you won't ride out of here when the sun comes up and never look back. Take time to rest and heal and to discover what's in your heart." Brenna touched his chest, then his forehead. "And what is in your head before you make a decision to leave or to stay." She held her breath for the answer that was slow in coming as he stood there looking at her.

"I can do that."

Satisfied, relieved, she said, "Good. Now, I'm going to finish cleaning up supper, then close the compound gates and go to bed. You've had a few hours more sleep than I have."

"Do what you need to in here. I'll close the gates."

"Thank you."

Matt paused at the end of the porch to roll a quirly then strike a match before he went on with the dogs following at his heels.

You know it's him—the brown-eyed man in your dreams. Don't worry. He'll stay.

"Will he?" Brenna tilted her head toward the whisper at her ear. "There is a journey yet before him that he must travel alone." She went to the table and opened the book at the ribbon to look again at the illustrations of the Wild Hunt. When she returned the book to the shelf, her fingers lingered on the spine while she stared into the darkness beyond the kitchen door. "And gold lies at the end of that journey. What happens then will either claim his life or free his soul."

***

Morning sounds brought Matt stretching and smiling from a restful sleep, and he rolled out of bed without undue groaning at the aches in his joints and muscles, then he dressed, and buckled on his gun belt. Inspecting his face in the mirror as he ran fingers through his hair, it looked like the knot on his forehead had gone down overnight, but it was still tender to touch.

He didn't find Brenna in the house, but fresh coffee and a pan of biscuits waited on the stove, so he helped himself on the way out the door. The sun's warmth breaking over Pine Mesa felt fine and fresh on his shoulders. The dogs ran circles around him, hoping he'd share his biscuits, and he didn't disappoint them. He reached the barn doors just as Brenna emerged with her egg basket in one hand and her shotgun in the other.

"Good morning, Matt."

Her smile warmed him more than the sunshine on his back. "'Mornin'."

"I hope you feel better than you did yesterday."

"I do. Thanks. Nothing like the healing tonic of sleep. The aching in my head is better, and I can see out of both of my eyes. My hands aren't so stiff, either. Whatever you rubbed on them did the trick."

Brenna looked him over with careful study that went from scrutinizing his face to inspecting his hands. "Yes. The swelling is down.

But your bruises are certainly a motley combination of colors. The gash across your cheek will probably scar. I'll treat it with my salve when we get to the house. So you slept well?"

He took the basket, and they walked across the compound yard together.

"Yeah, but I did some thinking last night."

"About what?"

"Couple of things."

"They must be important. You look so serious."

Seconds passed before he spoke. "I have to ask you something before we go any farther." A stab of guilt almost gave him away, but he kept a straight face and carried on. "I have to know..." He let out a heavy sigh.

"Yes? What is it?" Brenna placed her hand on his arm, encouraging him to continue.

"Brenna." He put on his best frown. "Did you take advantage of me when I was unconscious?"

The incongruity of his words in relation to what she'd been expecting was a lovely sight, and the smile he'd fought to suppress won the battle, and he grinned like a school boy winning at marbles.

A blush rose up her neck when she realized he was teasing, and she uttered a displeased *hrmpft* as she slapped a more than playful hit to his shoulder. "Matt Caddock. I thought you had something important to say. Of course, I didn't take advantage of you."

Laughing, he feigned a sore arm and rubbed the spot where she'd hit him. "But you thought about it, didn't you? Admit it."

Her eyes sparked with an ember of *I'll-get-even-for-this*. "That will always remain my secret." She picked up her pace and left him trotting to catch up.

"Hey, slow down." Chuckling at her little burst of temper, he snatched her hand and brought her to a halt. "I do have something serious to say."

She looked at him, her chin dipped, and her eyes still gleaming with the remnants of that little fire he'd ignited.

"I've drifted all my life. I need some time to get used to the idea of settling down in one place."

"What is your idea of an adequate length of time?"

"I don't know, but for starters, I'll work with your young horses and help out around the place. Help you haul in rocks for your paths. Mend tack. Whatever needs fixing. I'm a fair hand at that sort of work. And I wouldn't mind being here when your cattle arrive. It'd be a sight to witness a herd coming over the pass and spreading out on the rangeland." He shrugged. "After that, I'll play the hand that's dealt me."

Her chilly demeanor warmed with her smile, and he knew he was forgiven for teasing.

"Fair enough. Now, it's a hearty breakfast and out to begin a day's work for both of us."

Chapter Seven

"Matt! Come in for lunch!"

The clanging dinner triangle harkened him back to the last time he'd attended school and the teacher called the students to class the same way. He looked toward the sound although he couldn't see Brenna from where he was in the corral, and he imagined what it might be like to be called in like this every day. He didn't have to think about it for long to decide he could get used to it. Too used to it, too fast.

He beat the dust from his trousers then went to the windmill and cupped handfuls of water trickling from the pipe and splashed his face, then combed his fingers through his hair, wiped his face with a kerchief, and put his hat back on. As he crossed the yard, Brenna emerged from her house with the coffee pot in one hand and cups in the other. Too many years of living without a home lay along the wandering trail behind him, and the sight of Brenna in a bright summer dress with her long auburn braid swaying with her steps and the way her smile lit up her face when she saw him was a sight he'd hold in his memory until the day he took his last breath.

The summer table was already set with two places alongside a plate of cold meat from last night, a chunk of cheese, sliced bread, jar of pickles, and what looked and smelled like a freshly baked apple pie. His mouth started watering when he got a whiff of warm cinnamon spice when he sat down across from Brenna and put his hat on the bench beside him.

"How goes it with the colts?" Brenna poured coffee and filled glasses with water.

Matt forked meat, cheese, and bread onto a plate. "Good. You must have spent a lot of time with them. They're all three friendly as puppies, so most of the hard work is done. Today, we're just getting acquainted. Tomorrow, I'll put bits in their mouths then in a couple of days, I'll strap on saddle blankets. By the time I put saddles on them, I should be able to avoid blow-ups. They don't need to get the idea they can buck me off, besides it would hurt my pride."

He rubbed his backside in pseudo anguish, which brought head-shaking giggling from Brenna.

"Somehow, I doubt you'd get bucked off easily. I've watched you working with them. You have patience and a gentle way. I should have mentioned I named the roan filly Speckles and the sorrel colt Star because of the mark on his forehead. The bay colt is Dusty."

Matt nodded and took a swallow of coffee. "I'll remember that." Her blue eyes seemed even bluer and more inviting than they had last night.

"I did my own watching, and saw you working around the yard and tending the garden." He nodded toward the pie. "When you weren't baking."

Brenna glanced toward the kitchen garden. "I have plenty to do to stay busy, if that's what you mean. When Gregory and I came out here to help oversee the restoration, we hired a crew from Trinidad to handle the heavy construction. As you can see, there's still plenty of work to be done, but it's work we can do ourselves. It just takes time. We hired men to build the barbed-wire fences and put up the windmills, cut and haul in meadow hay, and bring down firewood from the mesas. That sort of work."

"That's a big expense."

"Yes, it is. There were no alternatives but to hire the work done."

"Well, you've done a fine job in a short time."

"Thank you. I think so, too. It's important to us that we're together and settled before Christmas."

"You say your rangeland is ready for the cattle?"

"Yes. The line shacks are stocked for the out riders and line riders this winter."

Matt looked around, pondering the amount of work they'd accomplished in such a short time. "How many head are coming in?"

"Upwards of four thousand. Mostly breeding stock."

Matt fumbled his cup. "Good God Almighty, Brenna."

Laughing, she wiped up the spill.

"How much land does your family own? I'm not a cattleman, but I do know to run cattle year round, you've got to have thirty or forty acres of good grass per animal in the best of years and supplement them with hay or some sort of feed. In dry years with hard winters, you need even more feed and grass, which means more acres and more expense to buy feed."

"My father's grandparents negotiated a seventy-thousand-acre land grant along with an agreement with the government to build this stockade for provisional military use. We've purchased another hundred-and-fifty-thousand. The land reaches south into the New Mexico Territory and north to the Arkansas River with some west of the Picketwire."

He whistled through his teeth. "Sounds like you come from a long line of money."

"No, not at all. It's a matter of luck and circumstances. I was born here, but I was quite young when we moved back east. We'd had an attack on the compound. I don't have my own memories of it, just the stories I've grown up with, and many of them are frightful. There was so much concern about the Comanche and Kiowa raiding this far north, and when it finally happened here, my parents took their young family back east where they felt it was safer.

"Charles and Mary, and Uncle Pete, my father's older brother, and Aunt Aggie stayed here to keep the buildings from falling into total disuse and abandonment. They ran a few head of cattle, traded with trappers, and with the friendly Indians, and received a monthly stipend from a stage company as a home stop on the route. Pete and Aggie never had children, so when Jim was old enough to travel alone, he returned here for the months when school wasn't on. My parents convinced Jim to get a college education before he moved here permanently. Young though we were when we left, Jim's heart has always been here." On a sigh, she added, "As has mine."

"So, back to when you left here. Where did you go?"

"To Philadelphia, with my mother's family. Secession was upon the land, and my father went to work for my grandparents in their carpentry business. When Gregory and I married, he wanted to contribute to our family plan to return here and build a cattle ranch, so he invested his inheritance. Regardless of the monetary contribution we all put in, we share and share alike in the profit and loss.

"We're not in the clear financially, though. My father borrowed a good deal of money for operating and living expenses as well as covering the cost of setting up several homes here. We have to make the money last until our first sale of cattle, which is at least two years away."

Matt nodded, thinking about all that entailed and what it meant for the entire Stirling family. "You've got a lot riding on a gamble. When you sell, I hope the market's in your favor."

"Yes, it is a huge gamble. We could easily lose everything. In fact, had it not been for a delay of several months in securing the additional money, we would have brought a herd here just in time for the awful winter of eighty-six and eighty-seven. Sometimes, what seems unfortunate at the time turns out to be a blessing in the long run."

Matt blew out a soft whistle. He'd seen with his own eyes the carcasses of animals that had frozen by the hundreds, even thousands, that winter.

They said little else while they finished eating, and Matt found he wasn't uncomfortable with the silence. It was good just sitting with her without the need for words. He sensed she felt the same. After a bit, he refilled their coffee while she cut the pie into quarters. She served him a quarter and cut a smaller piece for herself. Leaning close to the pie, he inhaled the aroma. When he finally took a mouthful, he held it without chewing, savoring the spices and apples all wrapped up in a tart-sweet flavor while trying to remember when anything had tasted this good.

Realizing Brenna was watching him, he sat up straighter, embarrassed. "That may have been the best thing I've ever eaten."

"I'm glad you liked it. Have more."

"It's tempting, but I'll wait until supper."

Brenna gathered their dishes and tableware and stacked them in the basket. "Supper is sometime between dusk and dark, and the coffee stays hot on the stove, so come in and help yourself. You'll always find pie or some other sweets."

Matt took her tidying up as an indication to get back to work, so he stood and put on his hat. "Thanks for lunch. I'm done with the horses for today. I'll oil all the saddles and tack this afternoon."

"Thank you. It's been on my mind to do, but I haven't found the time, other than for yours because it was soaked and muddy."

Matt strode back to the barn, and when he reached the wagon doors, he saw Brenna watching him, the basket handle over her arm and coffee pot in her grip. After a few more seconds, she went to her house, and he wondered what she'd been thinking. He'd like to believe he was the focus of her thoughts, especially after what she'd told him last night, but she hadn't mentioned that conversation today. As she'd said, daylight had a way of bringing truth and clarity to a person's thinking when a nighttime idea had seemed perfectly reasonable when it really wasn't. She'd probably had second thoughts, and he didn't blame her. He would, too, considering who he was.

Still, he wanted to believe what she'd said last night was sincere, but he was also a man who lived in reality. Besides, when you got to hoping for something too much, the disappointment when it *didn't* happen was hard to take.

***

After supper, Matt made one more pass around the compound and spent a few minutes at the corral with Socks before returning to the house. Ahead of him, silhouetted by the moon's light, Brenna walked to the house, her dressing gown fluttering around her legs, and her hair wrapped up in a towel. When he reached the porch, he stopped when he saw Brenna combing her hair, wet and a darker red, where it draped over her shoulder and reached nearly to her waist.

He'd never seen a woman comb her hair out before, wet or dry. It was a fascinating sight, alluring and evocative. He wondered what it would feel like to run his fingers through those silky damp tresses, and he imagined the fresh-washed aroma.

"You needn't wait for an invitation to come in."

Matt shook off his daydream and went inside. "I was watching you comb your hair. Don't stop on my account."

"I have three rules in my home that apply to everyone who stays here, including me."

"Those are?"

She pointed her comb at a folded towel with a razor, shaving cup and brush, and a bar of soap on the table. "A bath every night before bed."

Matt cocked his head and an eyebrow shot up. "A bath. Every night?"

"Yes. We have a bath house and laundry building across the yard. It was the only request I made when I returned here."

A frown worked its way over his face. "You want me to bathe every night."

"If you want to sleep in any of the beds in this house, yes. Or the option of staying in the bunkhouse stands. The hired help does their own laundry—and cooking, I might add—so I don't care how soiled their bed linens are."

Matt walked to the table that formed a barricade between them. Rubbing knuckles against his jaw, he said, "Well, taking a bath is a fair trade for the privilege of sleeping in a real bed and staying in your house. What are your other two rules?"

"Consideration and respect for others, as well as yourself. My parents instilled in all of their children the importance of good manners and helping one another. One must strive to practice those habits when living in an isolated place such as this."

"That's a good philosophy. What's the third?"

"Ask me another time."

"Why?"

"Because I asked you to." Brenna tossed the bar of soap, and he caught it. "There are clean clothes in your room."

Grinning, Matt said, "Yes, ma'am. I'll be sure to scrub behind my ears, too."

"You do that." Brenna returned his smile. "I'll meet you on the porch. It's a pleasant night to sit outside for a while."

Despite his slight annoyance at the thought of taking a bath every night, Matt warmed to the idea after soaking away the day's dust and sweat in the ample sized tub. He dressed and shaved, but kept the mustache Brenna had sculpted. Slinging his gun belt over his shoulder, he crossed the yard, his shirt unbuttoned, and the tail hanging loose.

"Drop your soiled clothing there." Brenna pointed to the corner of the porch. "Tomorrow is laundry day."

Matt deposited his dirty clothes where she'd indicated, then he sat in a chair beside her. "Do you miss your eastern life? There are a lot more conveniences for a woman there."

"That's true, but I brought many of them with me, and we're bringing in more all the time."

"From Trinidad?"

She nodded. "Colorado Springs, Denver, sometimes Santa Fé and Albuquerque."

"So you travel a lot. It's a fair distance to those cities."

"I've not gone farther than Trinidad since I moved here. I suppose I go into Trinidad three or four times a year to attend a performance at the Jaffa Opera House and to do a bit of shopping. I do love it here at the ranch, but I so miss music—concerts, operas, even church music."

She was silent for a few moments, and Matt watched a soft blanket of contentment settle upon her.

"It wasn't long after we moved here that I discovered sounds I'd not considered as music."

"What do you mean?"

"Wind rustling through the grasses, or humming through the pines and junipers or the cedars up on the hills. Birds singing their own special songs. Coyotes singing to the night. Crickets, toads." She sighed. "All I had to do was listen, and it was all around me."

He'd never thought of wind as musical. Mostly it grated on his nerves when it blew day after day, but it made sense once he thought about it. Even those daylight-clucking chickens had songs to sing.

Long after the moon's light turned from yellow to white, Matt held the kitchen door for Brenna, and he said goodnight as they went to their separate rooms. As he listened to the songs in the night, he wandered down the trail of his memories to a time when he'd felt a part of something more than his guns, his horse, and whatever was beyond the horizon. At the end of that trail was a childhood cut short. It wasn't a place he liked to visit, so he moved on and went to sleep.

Chapter Eight

"Brenna!" Matt left the bed in one frantic heart-pounding leap, sending the bedside table crashing. "Brenna!"

With a Colt clamped in his fist, he stood with his back to the far wall. Raking his gaze over every inch of the moonlit room, he searched the shadows and corners.

The door flew open. "Matt! What—" Whirling out of modesty, she put her back to him.

Matt made a catapulting leap onto the bed, snatched up his trousers, and grabbed Brenna's arm on his way out of the room. Hustling her along through the kitchen, he hit the porch door with such force it wedged open and ripped the cheesecloth from the upper half.

Words came fast as he pulled on his trousers while clutching his revolver. "Someone... A man. There was a man standing at the foot of my bed. One second he was there and the next he was gone. Just gone. What in hell fire was that? *Who* was that?"

"Gregory."

Comprehension arrived on frowning silence. "But...he's... Hell, you said he was dead. How could he be in that bedroom?" He shook his gun toward the door.

"That was our bedroom, and he died there. I changed bedrooms after he started visiting me in the night. I didn't think he would return to that bedroom once he began rocking in his chair by the fireplace. Obviously, I was wrong."

Matt stepped back, his gun arm lowering. "He rocks in a chair?" He blew out a slow, hard breath. "That's plumb crazy." Wagging a finger at her, he accused, "I think you've been alone out here too long. You've got a case of prairie madness."

Brenna crossed her arms. "Then we're *both* crazy. You saw him, too."

Staring across the yard, Matt opened his mouth, then clamped it shut. "Damn." Shoving his Colt into the waistband of his trousers, he went to the edge of the porch and stood in the doorway. Staring across the yard, he asked, "Has Jim seen him?"

"No, but he has seen the chair rocking."

Matt alternately nodded and shook his head, trying to make sense out of what was happening. Finally, he asked, "What about your dream...what you said about you and me?" He waved a hand in the air trying to pin down an elusive idea. "Have you told anyone?"

"Just Jim. I tell him everything."

Matt ran his fingers through his hair then rubbed his palms over his face.

"Would you like a drink? Other than wine, I have bourbon, rye, and brandy."

"Bourbon. Double."

Brenna lit the oil lamp on the kitchen table then the chink of glass-on-glass followed. Matt, taking in slow, deep breaths to calm his nerves, didn't hear her return until something cool touched his arm, and he jumped and twisted around with a yelp.

Brenna held out a glass of whiskey. "You're a little on the skittish side."

"You might say that, yeah." Matt swallowed his whiskey in two gulps.

"The bottle is on the kitchen table." Brenna went to her usual place on the wooden bench beside the kitchen door.

Matt shook his head. "I don't have much of a taste for whiskey. This was plenty."

She held her glass on her lap, cupping it with both hands. "You have questions. I owe you answers."

He did have questions, but right then, all he could muster was a hard swallow as he looked at her with her hair falling loose over her shoulders to lie upon her bosom. Her nightgown, although a modest covering, hinted at the curves of her womanly attributes beneath the light cotton material. Resting his hips against the porch railing, he needed to derail thoughts he'd no business thinking, so he waded right in.

"Tell me about him. About Gregory. Tell me about your marriage."

"All right. When I received my teaching certificate, my parents sent me on a holiday to Paris and London to celebrate. Music was my passion, and all my life I'd dreamed of seeing an opera in Paris.

As it happened, the first night I attended the Garnier Opera House, I was introduced to Gregory Gérard. We met often in the weeks that followed before I returned to London and then back to America. A few months of exchanging letters ensued, and before a year had passed, Gregory came to Philadelphia and asked for my hand in marriage."

She was quiet for a few moments. "He possessed the most generous, kind nature. He was musically gifted and highly intelligent, but he'd led a quiet, sheltered life that he said lacked purpose or true meaning. He said he'd found his reason for living when we met, and he loved me with all his heart. He was a good, steady partner. More than that, he was a good man. We shared so many interests. Music, literature, theater. I loved him, in my own way."

Something in her tone sounded incomplete, regretful. "What way was that?"

Brenna circled a finger around the rim of her glass. "Dearly, but not passionately. Not for all time."

"Did he know you felt that way?"

"Yes."

Matt considered that idea and decided he didn't care for it. "That was an agreeable arrangement?"

Brenna shrugged. "Yes. Quite satisfactory."

"It seems a little one-sided in his favor."

Brenna smiled. "I suppose it was. You see, he was dying, but we didn't know it at the time. We'd been married a few months when the illness he'd struggled with since childhood returned after a long period of dormancy."

"What was wrong with him?"

"He suffered from a little understood chronic disease that has a long and scientific name, but doctors call it *lupus*. Since early childhood, he'd had occurrences of a rash that spread over his cheeks that was accompanied by his bone joints swelling and aching so much he could hardly move about. Fatigue often left him prostrate in bed for days. As he grew older, being in the sunlight for any length of time made his condition worse, and then for no reason he could discern, he'd not have symptoms for months.

"A year or so passed, and we returned to his family's estate in France to claim his inheritance and to pursue medical care with a Viennese physician who accepted Gregory as a special study patient. We stayed in Europe two years. Despite this doctor's expertise, Gregory's health deteriorated, and he chose to return to America. It was important to him that I shouldn't be so far from my family when he died."

Matt dragged a well-worn rocking chair in front of her and sat down. "Apparently, he lived a while longer."

"He did. The excitement and the work involved to make the move to Colorado was a boon to his determination to keep his illness at bay. Once again, the symptoms subsided." Brenna closed her eyes.

Matt wondered if the little frown worrying her forehead was from missing her husband or from the feelings of hopelessness of his condition and watching him die. Both were emotions he knew himself, and he said as much.

"I was with my pa at my ma's bedside when she passed on. She took sick with a fever and died a few days later. When you can't do anything to help but sit by and wish it wasn't so, it leaves a mean, empty feeling inside that you can never shake off."

Brenna nodded. "Yes. Yes, it does."

Matt chanced an observation. "You never had children."

Brenna said nothing for many seconds then opened her eyes and stared at her whiskey glass. "Twice, we had hopes, but I barely carried into the third month."

"That's hard. You wish you had children, don't you?"

"I used to, but I've accepted that this house will not hear children's laughter."

He stared at his feet, thinking about what children meant to a woman. When he looked at her, he saw the shine of unshed tears in her eyes.

"But sometimes you still wish."

With a hasty wipe at her eyes, she nodded.

"Are you...are you still mourning him?"

"No. I've let go of Gregory."

"But he hasn't let go of you."

"He will. He's just watching over me until he knows I won't be alone."

"You're not alone. You've got family."

Brenna shrugged. "Yes, but it's more than that. You and Gregory are linked in a way I've never understood. The day we married, I looked into Gregory's eyes, and I saw yours. It was as if Gregory was a portal to another place in time—a place and time where you existed. At that moment, and then later in dreams, our three lives merged as if everything in our pasts came forward to the present and joined us in the future. Gregory looked for omens and portents in all aspects of life, and they guided his decisions and influenced his beliefs."

"So, he was superstitious."

She shook her head. "No. Not at all. He was... sensitive. Aware and intuitive. In that, we were alike, which is why I believe when he speaks to me from his otherworld, I'm able to hear him, or perhaps more than hear, I feel him, his presence."

"Is he still in the bedroom?"

Brenna lifted her chin and tilted her head. After a few moments, she relaxed and shook her head. "No. I have no sense of him here."

Matt sawed his hand across the back of his neck, trying to make sense out of this. "Help me understand something. If he's been waiting for me to show up so you won't be alone, why is he still here?"

"I've wondered that, too. Perhaps he has an unfinished task to complete before his spirit can rest. I just don't know."

Hedging, Matt said, "I've got to ask you something you may not like."

"All right. What?"

"We're talking about ghosts and spirits and whatever might be out there in the afterlife, if there is one. Have you ever considered he might not be what you think he is?"

"You mean a nasty spirit intending to do harm or mischief?"

"Something along that line, yeah."

Her slight smile softened her already serene features. "No. There is nothing evil or threatening in Gregory's presence, only love and a desire for my well-being."

Appeased for the time being, Matt asked, "Do you still have that dream?"

"Oddly enough, the dream ceased upon Gregory's death. I like to think he took the dream with him. With his last words, he promised to watch over me until you arrived. Of course, I didn't take him literally. But I accepted those words into my heart as a comfort that his memory would be with me, always. Then, he went to sleep and didn't awaken. He died a few hours later." Brenna swirled what was left of her whiskey. "It was on his urging that I rode to the creek. He knew I'd find you there."

Matt rocked forward and planted his feet on the porch floor. "Brenna, seeing him standing at my bedside scared the daylights out of me."

"You don't have to continue sleeping in that room."

He thought he was back on solid ground, but the invitation in her eyes threw him off-stride. "Do you have a specific room in mind?"

"I have a third bedroom or, perhaps, you'll join me in mine...when the time is right."

"But that time isn't now?"

She shook her head. "If the stars in our eyes tonight still shine as the days go by, we'll know when."

"You're a woman full of surprises and mystery. I'll say that for you." Matt stood and offered his hand. "One thing, though. Your husband—Gregory. Does he do anything else in that bedroom? I mean, does he just stand beside the bed?"

Brenna giggled. "He lingers, and then he leaves. That's all."

"Well, then, I'll introduce myself next time he shows up and invite him to sit a spell."

Returning his smile, Brenna said, "I'm sure he'll appreciate your hospitality. Good night, Matt."

"Good night, Brenna."

Chapter Nine

By the end of another long week, Matt had taken the two colts and the filly for their first excursion outside of the corral. Brenna had ridden along, snubbing each horse to Samson, who was as easy-going and level-headed as he was strong. At fifteen hands at his withers, combined with his even temperament, it made him a good horse for breaking colts to ride.

Snubbing kept the young horses from bolting, and it discouraged bucking, while also serving to drag them along until they figured out they were supposed to keep up. Matt and Brenna covered enough ground going away from the compound that on the return trip, the colts and filly were tired enough for Matt to ride them independently of the snubbing rope.

In a few more days, Matt rode each one out alone. On one of those days, he'd just turned Speckles into the corral when he spied two riders coming up the road long before the dogs ran off barking to greet them. Ducking into the barn, he stayed in the shadows where they couldn't see him and slipped the thongs off the hammers of his revolvers. Brenna met the visitors at her porch step, her shotgun cradled in the crook of her arm with barrel pointed down, but in their general direction.

The cowboys tipped their hats, careful to keep their hands in plain sight. One man glanced over his shoulder, which indicated to Matt they'd seen him in the corral and were wondering where he was. That was all right with him. It kept a man from making a wrong move when he didn't know who might have a gun aimed at his midsection.

"Howdy, ma'am."

"Hello, gentlemen. I never turn away an injured or hungry man. Help yourself to water and cool yourselves in the shade over there." She waved toward the summer table. "But if your intentions are otherwise, I invite you to leave now in the same healthy condition as when you arrived."

Matt smiled when she lifted the shotgun barrel a few inches to make her not-so-subtle point.

"Thank you, ma'am. I promise, we mean no ill toward you. I expect you're Mrs. Gérard?"

"Yes. What is your business?"

"We just come through Trinidad headed to Laramie, and we offered to deliver these letters to you." He reached inside his vest and brought out two letters. The cowboy dismounted, handed his reins to his partner, and walked to Brenna.

Matt crossed the yard, keeping close to the buildings, and though neither cowboy looked toward him, Matt knew from the glances they exchanged they were aware of his approach.

"Thank you. That was thoughtful, but also considerably out of your way."

"Our pleasure, and we don't mind." The cowboy took a respectful step back. "To be honest, we could have been here yesterday, but we'd heard tell you make bear sign—doughnuts—on Sunday mornings, so we waited. And word got to us that the postmaster was looking for someone comin' this way who would bring letters and..." The cowboy ducked his head, turning his hat in his hands like it was a wagon wheel rolling along.

Brenna smiled at his confession. "I do have doughnuts. They're still warm. I'll bring them to the table along with coffee and milk. Make yourselves at home."

Matt recognized the men. "Akins. Myerson. Been a long time."

Both men turned to him. Akins, the cowboy who'd done the talking asked, "Caddock? Matt Caddock? Well, I'll be damned." He shot a sheepish look toward Brenna. "Sorry, ma'am." He held out his hand, and Matt shook it. "How did you end up here? Last we heard, you'd taken an arrow somewhere up in the high country. Also heard you hooked up with Archer."

"You heard right on both, but I got shut of him."

Akins pushed back the front of his hat, nodding. "I hear what you're sayin'. He's runnin' a mean game. Story is, he blew a section of tracks down around Lamy for the payroll on the train. Waited until dark and wasn't ridin' a horse anyone recognized. Looks like he got away with it."

Myerson added, "Watch your back trail. Couple of fellas in Trinidad said they'd heard Archer'd headed down toward Big Spring looking for you." He dismounted and shook Matt's hand.

"Thanks for the warning. He and his boys worked me over down in Maxwell a while back. I left them wishing they hadn't."

"Well, now that you're shut of him, best stay that way. Archer kills just for sport, and he likes the sound of big explosions."

"That, he does. Always made me nervous that he carried a couple of sticks of dynamite in his saddlebags, though I never was around when he used them. I'd appreciate you not mentioning you saw me here, or anywhere else."

"That road runs both ways."

Matt nodded that he understood.

The men drank their fill of coffee and milk and, between them, ate a plate full of doughnuts before riding off with more doughnuts tied-up in an old tea towel. Matt waited until the riders were well away from the compound gates before speaking what was on his mind.

"Archer's got fever for easy gold, and he won't stop looking until he finds me." He drew his gaze from the riders to look at Brenna. "I should leave. Now."

Her chin came up, and her shoulders straightened. "Do what you feel you must."

Damn her blue eyes.

"As long as I'm here, you're in danger."

"I've handled danger before this."

Matt exhaled hard. "Not like Archer."

"Then describe him, so I'll know when, or if, he stops in."

"He'll have two or three men with him, and he'll be riding a flashy horse. Probably a big, rawboned sorrel paint. He's near my height and build. His eyes are narrow, deep-set, and he wears his hair longish. He'll have two guns strapped on, high and backward—for a border draw." He demonstrated what he meant.

Brenna frowned, a mocking expression if he'd ever seen one, with her head tilted as she looked him over.

"It seems to me a man isn't much of a shot if he can't hit what he's shooting at with one gun."

Matt looked down at his double holsters then back to her, chuckling at her joshing. "There's truth in that, sure enough, but two guns has kept me and Archer alive this far. Cuts down on reloading time. Archer blasts away and sheer luck makes enough bullets hit the mark that he's gotten a reputation as being plumb *loco* with a shooting iron."

"What about you? How do you shoot?"

"With deliberate intent. I don't miss what I aim at."

Her teasing smirk faded, and he saw in her eyes that she understood the difference between him and Archer.

"Why did you throw in with him?"

It took him a few seconds to get his thoughts around how to explain. "Sometimes, a man finds himself with strange companions. Henry always said to take care of my friends, but to keep a closer watch on my enemies...if I'm lucky enough to know who they are. At the time, it was safer for Archer and me to be on the same side than against each other. And, I got him out of a tough spot in Waco, so he was beholden to me. It made him a better riding partner, because he owed me."

"That seems rather short-lived appreciation, since he turned on you in Maxwell."

"Loyalty isn't one of his attributes." He looked at her a good long while. "If he shows up here... Well, don't be caught without a weapon, and don't wait too long to use it."

"I won't, but neither will I fret and flap waiting for him to show up."

He should leave. His head told him to light out and not look back, but his heart turned a deaf ear. There was no place else he wanted to be except here with Brenna. "We'll keep a keen eye on the land from now on. When visitors pass through, I'll stay out of sight until we know their intentions."

"Good. A simple plan is the best plan. Now, let's go in and open the letters."

Matt helped himself to a glass of water, then sat across from Brenna at the kitchen table, enjoying the myriad of expressions crossing her face as she read. When she finished the first letter, she slid it to him.

"You might be interested in this one. It's from Jim."

Matt picked up the letter, and Brenna explained it while he read, which amused him, but he let it go. She was excited, and he like the way her eyes lit up as she talked.

"It's dated a month ago. He says they started with forty-two hundred head and hopes to reach here with at least four thousand after they cut some out as payment for crossing private land and from natural loss on the trail. He says the grass is good, water is plenty, and they're making slow and steady progress, and the cattle aren't losing weight."

Matt read through Jim's letter for the rest of the details, while she read the other to herself.

When she finished, she said, "This is from Grandma Mary. Listen to this. 'Our plans have changed. We are still in Denver and awaiting a delayed shipment, which we will accompany to Trinidad by train then freight by wagon to the ranch. Don't look for us to return before the latter part of August at the very earliest. I do hope this delay doesn't cause you worry, and I am sorry you have so much work yet to finish while Charles and I are not there to help. Charles has fished every day regardless of the weather, and I may never get him out of the river to come home. It has been a well-needed and well-deserved holiday for him. I have enjoyed being in the city, but I miss the ranch, your bright cheerful smile, and your delightful voice when you sing.

"'While Charles has been hip-deep in river water, I've enjoyed shopping for all of us. Not only have I purchased the loveliest bolt cloth, I've also purchased a case each of two of the French wines you so love. We're bringing the latest design in cook stoves and wood stoves, new washing machines, ice boxes, light fixtures, furniture, tableware, metal screen for the windows and porch doors, clocks, brooms, mops, bed linens, pillows, rugs, and so much more that the list would be more than I have paper to write on. We've made do with second-hand goods long enough. Just imagine the time Dara will have setting-up her new home with Jim between now and the wedding.

"'You can see from this stationery we have rooms at the Albany Hotel, so when you have a few free minutes, which I know are rare and precious, please send a letter and tell us how you're getting on...'"

Brenna re-read the rest of the letter in silence, smiling to herself and twirling the end of her braid between her fingers. She was the prettiest woman Matt had ever known, especially when she smiled, and she smiled a lot. He could sit there all day and just watch her. After a bit, he refolded Jim's letter, stuffed it into the envelope, and put his hat on.

Pushing back from the table, he said, "I'm going to take a ride out to the creek to look for my hat, and I need to put a few miles on Socks or he's liable to buck me off with all the orneriness he's stored up since we got here."

"I have lunch dishes to wash and a letter to begin. I'll add a few lines each day until I can send it with someone passing through on the way to Trinidad."

As he stepped off the porch, Brenna's voice lifted in song of green growing lilacs, and he hummed a few bars along with her as he strode to the barn.

Chapter Ten

Matt returned to the compound an hour before dark under a light sprinkle that had the feel of a full-blown rain behind it. Brenna waved from the porch, and he rode to her, noticing she wore her hair pulled back with a ribbon instead of plaited. He liked the difference, while thinking how pretty she was no matter how she wore her hair.

Reining in, he tossed his borrowed hat to her then removed his recovered hat from his head, looked it over for a second, and put it back on. "It was about half-a-mile from where I fell into the creek. When the water receded, it stuck in a tangled mess of debris. It's in better shape than I expected."

"I'm glad you found it. Supper is stew and johnny cake whenever you're hungry."

"I'll put Socks up and give him a bait of grain then be right in."

"Chores are done other than shutting up the chickens for the night. I'll be out in a few minutes to do that."

Matt grained Socks, rubbed him down then put away the saddle, blanket, and bridle. Sprinkles turned to light rain, and he went to the barn door and looked at the clouds. Brenna was part way to the barn when the clouds opened and rain peppered straight down. Instead of running for shelter, she stretched out her arms and twirled in circles, her smiling face turned to the sky. One of the dogs jumped up, and she grabbed his paws, dancing and laughing as he hopped along on his hind legs. Lightning flashed and thunder answered, which sent dogs scampering ahead of her in her sprint to the barn.

"Out there with the dogs, you looked like a little girl who sneaked away to play in the creek in her Sunday clothes. You're soaked."

Giggling, Brenna looked down at herself. Her hand flew to her chest where the cloth stuck to her skin, accentuating her cleavage. She jerked her head up, her eyes wide, and embarrassment dark on her cheeks. He caught her gaze, held it, and took a step closer. Reaching behind her neck, he pulled her hair ribbon loose and drew it along her shoulder then let it slip through his fingers.

"Don't cover yourself."

He liked the way she looked—wet and self-conscious—but not so much as to turn from him. He put a hand over hers and tugged gently for her to release the grip she had on her blouse. She lowered her arms. Matt made slow work of trailing his gaze from her face to her bosom where the wet cloth did little to conceal the tantalizing curve of her breasts.

"You were wearing this blouse when you pulled me from the creek. You look mighty fetching in yellow, especially when you're wet." He drew his gaze up with some effort. "Shake your hair out."

Brenna dipped her chin and gave her hair a shake, sending cool, damp sprinkles splashing his face. Short curly tendrils framed her face. He wanted to bury his hands in her hair, wrap his arms around her, and kiss her full lips again. Her breasts, rising and falling with her rapid, shallow breathing, teased and tempted him to explore their hidden treasures beneath the wet cloth.

"You are more woman than any woman I've ever known. Just looking at you begs a man to kiss you." He exhaled a slow, ragged breath. "And if I kiss you again, I won't want to stop there."

She whispered, "I won't want you to stop."

Matt lifted an arm, hesitated, then sank his fingers into her thick, damp hair and lifted a handful to his face to breathe in the soapy clean aroma he'd imagined. When she slid her hands down his sides and along his hips, he sucked in a breath, anticipating her destination. Instead, she grasped both sides of his gun belt at the buckle, and the glint in her eyes promised mischief of a sort he was more than ready to engage in.

Cocking his head, he warned, "Be damned sure you want me, because if my gun belt comes off, so do your clothes."

"If my clothes come off, that means you've decided to stay."

He forgot about his violent past. He pushed away doubts that all he had to offer was what he'd arrived with, which was shamefully little. All he wanted in his life was this woman.

"For you, I'd tackle hell in my bare feet with a bucket of water and a Bible."

He untied the holster strings around his thighs by feel, and she eased his gun belt to the ground. A little smirk played at her mouth as she undid the top button of her blouse, then the next, and the next before he pushed her hands aside and finished the tantalizing task only to come face-to-face with a barricade he didn't know how to breach snugged down over a sleeveless, thin white garment.

"Good Lord, how many layers do you have on?"

Her words came on a delighted giggle. "Not enough to hinder us."

She unhooked down the front of the corset barricade, and the offending garment fell open. A line of tiny pearl buttons on her chemise beckoned him. He worked open the top two buttons, her skin cool and damp against his fingers.

Patience with the buttons reached an end. "To hell with this."

Running his hands inside her open blouse and up her bare arms, he brought the blouse over her shoulders and down her back to let it hang loose from the waist of her skirt. She pulled her arms free of her sleeves and tossed his hat aside as he pushed her backward until she came up against the wooden planks of a stall. Fumbling together and laughing at their mutual eagerness, they managed to bunch up handfuls of her skirt, and he groped at her undergarments, relieved he didn't encounter a challenge he couldn't overcome, while she worked with nimble fingers to unbutton his trousers. Her hands were all over him, inside his shirt, tugging his trousers down.

It was awkward, but he certainly didn't care, and she wasn't complaining. He had a fleeting stab of guilt that she deserved more than a roll in the hay here in the barn, but her fingers dug into his shoulders and her tongue found his ear, sending those thoughts right out of his mind.

Lightning lit up the sky; thunder crackled. The tempest building inside Matt surged and peaked with Brenna that seemed to shake the ground beneath their feet. Resting his forehead against the panel while his ragged breathing eased, he encircled Brenna's waist with one arm to hold her trembling body as support for them both.

When he could talk, he asked, "Where...where do we go from here? What happens now?"

Brenna's arms tightened around his shoulders, and she turned her face to his cheek to place a whisper of a kiss there. "I have a bottle of wine and a soft bed." She put her hands upon his chest and pushed him back to see his face. "I'd like to share them both with you."

He looked at her a good long while before he answered. "Just for tonight?"

"Tonight, tomorrow, or fifty years. I'll cherish however long we have."

He'd never thought of his life in forever terms before, and he decided right then, he'd like to give it a try.

***

Matt opened his eyes to darkness. Withdrawing a revolver from his gun belt hanging on the bedpost, he ran the unfamiliar noise around in his head, separating it from the gentle patter of rain while drawing upon his cache of sound-memories with no success in pinning it down. As he lay still listening, he recalled falling to sleep with Brenna in his arms, which brought a smile. Since he'd moved into her bedroom, she'd nearly worn him out, but he couldn't think of a better way to spend his nights.

Reaching for her, all he found was the impression of where she'd been. Surmising she was the source of the noise, he holstered his gun, and pulled on his trousers. A few steps into the common room, he paused and surveyed both kitchen and living room, but all he picked out were shadowy shapes in the darkness. Then he realized the rocking chair was moving.

He crossed the cool stone floor in bare feet to the high-backed wooden rocking chair that faced the fireplace. "Brenna? Why are you out here?" He stepped around to the front of the chair.

It was empty.

Back and forth it went in a slow, even motion with the rockers making the regular grinding noise he'd heard. His mouth went dry; the back of his neck tingled. His hands moved toward his guns. *Shit.* They were in the bedroom right alongside his Winchester. Hell's Bells. He couldn't shoot a ghost, anyway.

Backing toward the kitchen, he called for Brenna in a low tone that still sounded too loud in the moonless night.

"Out here, Matt."

He took no time leaving the house. Standing in front of Brenna, he pointed over her shoulder, "The chair...there's a chair inside rocking. And there's no one in it." Was he stating a fact or asking for reassurance?

"I know. That's what woke me. I'd hoped it would stop before you heard it."

"How long does he—" Matt swallowed hard. "How long will it keep rocking?" He felt foolish admitting a ghost was rocking in that chair.

"Sometimes all night. Other times, just a few minutes."

"Maybe you should move into one of the other houses—or build a new house."

From her place on the bench beside the door, she sighed as she toyed idly with the ends of her hair. "I don't really mind, especially since I changed bedrooms."

"Then take the chair out. Store it somewhere."

She shook her head. "My father made the chair for Gregory during one of the long spells when his illness kept him housebound. To hide it seems disrespectful to his memory. He'll move on when he's ready, or when he's able."

"Well, if you can handle him staying around, I guess I can, too." He knelt in front of her and rubbed his hands up and down her bare arms. "You're cold. How long have you been out here?"

"Half-an-hour, I suppose." She inhaled a deep breath. "Doesn't the air smell wonderful?"

For a few seconds, he turned his attention to the drizzle and the other night sounds, trying to ignore the monotonous rocking in the house. Taking hold of her hands, he brought her up and into his arms. "Let me warm you up."

"*Mmm.* That's nice."

She rested her head upon his chest, and he pressed his cheek against her hair, as he took a few slow, shuffling steps.

"What are you doing?"

"Dancing." He made a sliding step then another, moving them in a small circle.

She looked up at him, her eyebrows furrowed in question. "There's no music."

He kissed the juncture of her frown. "Close your eyes and listen. Can't you hear the music in the rain pattering on the porch roof and the sputtering it makes when it splashes into the mud, and the tinny plinks of rain drops on the windmill?"

After a moment, she said, "Yes. I do hear the music."

They continued their gentle dance and, after a bit he said, "Brenna."

"*Hmm?*"

"What's your third rule?"

"Only love is allowed to come into this home and stay."

She lifted her head, and he saw something he'd never seen in a woman's eyes—love for him. And he knew he loved her, too.

"I need to marry you. I want to."

Something flickered in her eyes. Maybe doubt, or even regret. Whatever it was, seeing it set him back and a twinge of hurt rose tight and hot in his throat. "You don't believe me. Or...you don't want to marry me?"

She barely shook her head. "I believe you. But I don't need that right now."

"Will you ever need it?"

"Someday. When the time is right." Sighing, she rested her head against his chest, and whispered, "When the time is right for us both.

"When will we know?"

"I don't know. We just will."

For many minutes, Matt held her, hardly moving, yet gently swaying to the night music.

"The rocking has stopped."

Matt cocked an ear toward the kitchen door. Next time Gregory showed up, he'd have a talk with him about Brenna. Man-to-man, or man-to-spirit. That thought sent a chill down his back, but he'd tell Gregory his feelings toward Brenna were honest, and maybe that would ease his restless spirit. He sure hoped it would. Ghostriders were enough to deal with. He didn't need Brenna's dead husband after him, too.

***

August wore its heat well, and the first of September arrived with the promise of an early autumn. It was a late afternoon when Matt watched Brenna traverse the rock path with the joyous, light-hearted steps of a school girl playing hopscotch or four-square with her braid bouncing and the wide brim of her gardening hat flopping. The footpath wound in and around bushes, flowers, and saplings that, as they grew, would offer much-appreciated shade over the front and west side of each house.

Grinning and a little out of breath, she trotted to him. "So, what do you think? Does it look nice?"

He put his arm across her shoulders. "Yes, it does. You've worked hard on it. You should be proud."

"As a matter-of-fact, I am." She puffed up, and he laughed at her put-on self-importance. "I won't be able to start the next project until Grandpa and Grandma return with the supplies, though."

Matt pecked her cheek with a quick kiss. "Walk with me." They headed toward the compound gates. "Looks to me like you have about ten minutes to wait. I've been watching them through field glasses for the past hour." What he didn't say was Archer was never out of his thoughts, which kept him on a constant vigil for signs of travelers.

"Watching whom?" Brenna shaded her eyes against the glare of the setting sun. In a rush of wagging tails and exuberant barking, the dogs charged toward the caravan coming up the last mile.

"I figured with that big of an outfit, it had to be your grandparents, and there are others with them."

Brenna sucked in a gasp. "They're all here!" she breathed. "My parents are here!" Brenna shook his arm in her excitement then gathered handfuls of her skirt and took off running.

An uneasy feeling took hold in the pit of his stomach. He'd never met a woman's parents before, but one thing he knew was they tended to question a man's intentions toward their little girls, no matter how grown-up those little girls were—especially the fathers. He decided right then he'd rather walk down the main street of Dodge City without his guns and wearing nothing but women's drawers than to meet Brenna's parents and explain why he slept in her bed when he wasn't her husband.

Damn.

Chapter Eleven

Freight wagons, buckboards, and buggies rolled into the yard, and Brenna jumped down from the seat of the lead buckboard and ran about hugging and kissing her family and circling back amongst them to do it all again. Chattering and laughter rose over a cacophony of voices.

Matt enjoyed the reunion happiness from an unobtrusive position. Since the death of his mother, he'd never been around a family, and if he had grandparents, he didn't know who they were or where they lived. As an only child, he'd missed out on knowing a sibling relationship. It was clear this group was as close-knit as they came. When Brenna spied him in his out-of-the-way spot near the windmill, she hurried to him.

"Now is not the time to be shy. Come with me." She grasped his hand and led him toward the wagons.

He regretted they hadn't talked about this moment, about meeting her family, but it was too late to worry. He had to tough it out. The one thing set in his mind was if Brenna's family didn't cotton to him, they'd have to find a way to at least tolerate him. He wasn't leaving here without her, and he'd never ask her to leave, so an agreement of some sort had to be reached.

Brenna made the introductions. "Matt, these are my parents, James and Ann Stirling. My grandparents, Charles and Mary Stirling. Aunt Aggie Stirling. This is Dara Everett, my brother Jim's fiancée. Her family lives about ten miles from us on the way to Trinidad. Jim and Dara are getting married at Christmastime. And this is my little brother, Andrew. We call him Drew."

Impulsively, she hugged Drew for the umpteenth time Matt had observed.

"And you're not so little anymore."

His cheeks reddened, but he puffed out his chest. "Thanks, Brenna."

Matt nodded in greeting with each introduction. When Brenna paused to catch her breath, he stepped up to her father and offered his hand.

"Matt Caddock, sir."

James took his hand with a firm grasp. "Pleased to meet you. Call me James."

Matt held his hand out to Charles, who greeted him with an open, friendly smile and handshake. "I answer to Charles and my friends call me Charlie. Choose what makes you comfortable."

"Yes, sir."

Ann stepped forward and wrapped Matt in a motherly embrace before he saw it coming. He lifted his arms to return her embrace, but could only bring himself to pat her lightly on the back before he extricated himself.

"It's so nice to meet you, Matt. James and I certainly appreciate that you've been here with Brenna. We've worried about her being alone, and it was such a relief to find out that wasn't the case. Thank you."

"Nice to meet you Mrs. Stirling." He tipped his hat to her, wary about how smoothly this was progressing and uneasy that they weren't surprised he was living here. Then he realized he needed to greet the other women, and the situation fell apart as he muddled on, sounding like an idiot and feeling like one, too. "Pleased to meet you Mrs. Stirling, Mrs. Stirling, and Miss...almost Mrs. Stirling."

Ann's laughter, as rich and melodious as Brenna's didn't help Matt's embarrassment.

"That won't do at all. You must use first names, Matt."

Drew piped up before Matt had time to crawl deeper into the hole he'd dug for himself, and from which he saw no escape.

"Are you really a gunfighter like in the dime novels? Grandma showed us the letter Brenna wrote. She told all about you. Papa says we need to be polite because you're Brenna's friend. I think it's because you might shoot us if you don't like us."

Brenna whipped around, aghast. "Drew—"

James interjected, "Andrew Charles Stirling. That's quite enough. Apologize to—"

Matt waved him off. "No harm done." He half-knelt, half-stooped to eye level with Drew, working not to smile at the boy's round-eyed fright.

"How old are you? Twelve? Thirteen?"

"Thir...thirteen just last month."

Matt continued to study him. "I like your honesty, Drew. If you're man enough to say out loud what you're thinking, then always mean what you say and stick by it. But don't be hurtful or a braggart, or someone will feed your words back to you." He cut a glance toward James. "I *am* a gunfighter, but more importantly, I'm Brenna's friend. I'd never hurt her or anyone she loves. I'll do everything I can to protect them."

Drew exhaled the breath he'd been holding, and a big smile broke over his face. "Whew! I was worried all the way from Denver that you wouldn't like us, and that I'd made the trip from Philadelphia just to get shot."

Standing and laughing, Matt held out his hand. Drew shook it vigorously. Then Matt faced the family group, feeling back in control and ready to take charge.

"I'll bet you're all hungry and ready to wash off the dust from the road. How about we get acquainted over supper and unload tomorrow?"

James gave an approving nod. "Splendid idea. We'll unpack the few things we need for tonight. I'll speak with the freighters and have them stay in the bunkhouse. It's too late for them to return to Trinidad tonight, even if we unloaded now."

"I'll give a hand," Matt offered.

"Brenna, shall we prepare supper in your house?" Mary asked.

"Certainly. Go on in. I'll be right along. We'll gather at the summer table." Brenna turned to Matt. "You handled that well."

Matt gave her his best *I-don't-like-surprises* frown. "You might have told me they already knew I was here."

Brenna chewed her bottom lip, cringing just a little. "We're not very good at keeping secrets in this family."

"Do they know I stay with you? I can't think that any of them will look favorably on us sleeping in the same bed, given we haven't made it legal."

"You worry too much. They won't think twice about where we sleep."

"How do you know?"

"I've told you about my brother, Jim." Her lips pursed in a self-satisfied smirk.

"Yeah."

"Have I mentioned he's my twin, and that my parents lived here, together, but didn't marry until we were three years old and my mother was expecting my sister?" She kissed his cheek, turned on her heels, and laughed delightedly on her way to the house.

Matt stared at her. *I'll be damned.* Chuckling at her ornery streak that showed up now and again, he shook his head, muttering, "No, Brenna. You didn't mention that."

***

Over supper, Matt listened more than joined in with the reunion conversation. He was content sitting beside Brenna and watching each person in order to get a feel for their individual personalities and behaviors. He saw Brenna's straightforward manner in her mother and the same auburn hair, but her blue eyes were her father's. Ann's fine breeding, sophistication, and education showed in her every aspect, and she'd certainly passed those attributes on to Brenna.

He heard about Brenna's younger sister, Corrine, who had earned her medical license, but wasn't moving here until closer to the first of the year. Her head was set on bettering the medical care for women and children in this part of the country. Drew interjected periodically with his own colorful stories of the journey west.

Putting the family chatter aside, what Matt really discovered and what he admired—even envied—was their devotion to each other and their determination to make a go of ranching. Their single-minded plan over the last three years had been to reunite by Christmas, and their diligence had brought them together months before.

This brought to the forefront what had been rolling around in the back of his mind for weeks. What did he have to contribute to Brenna? To her family? All he possessed was his fast guns, a strong back, and the belief his pa had instilled in him that a man had to pull his own weight if he was any kind of man at all.

Right then, it started to eat at him that he was coming up short in his pa's eyes.

***

By daylight, Brenna had coffee brewing and biscuits baking, and it wasn't long before the compound bustled with the work of unloading. Everywhere she looked traveling trunks, luggage, and untold numbers of boxes and crates that held personal and household items, groceries, and sundry ranch supplies decorated the yard. Furniture, bedding, stoves and other domestic machines awaited assignment to their permanent locations. She was particularly pleased with the sets of McGuffy Readers and box of slate boards to continue Drew's education and for other children who lived close enough to ride or walk to the compound for schooling.

By noon, only the large wooden railroad shipping crate remained in the back of a freight wagon. It took some doing, but the men hand-maneuvered the wagon to Brenna's porch, and let down the loading ramp at the back. Brenna looked from the smiling faces of family members to the crate then over to Matt who just shrugged and shook his head.

Hands on her hips, she asked, "What is this?"

Ann held out a flat leather case. "The answer to your question is inside."

She untied the strings on the front, lifted the flap, and peered inside. "It's sheet music."

"Yes. We also brought tuning instruments and a cabinet in which to store the music."

Slow to grasp her mother's meaning, Brenna stared at the crate for many seconds before realization came to her. "This...this...is a piano? You brought a piano?"

"And it's brand new." Ann hugged Brenna. "We knew how much you missed music. We've been in Denver for three weeks waiting for it to arrive from Chicago. I insisted we couldn't leave without it."

"I...I don't know what to say." Brenna wiped her eyes with her apron hem. Smiling through happy tears, she embraced her father. "Thank you. I have just the place for it."

Once situated in the place of honor along the wall at the juncture of the kitchen and living room, Brenna ran a dust cloth with a loving touch over the piano's dark polished wood.

"I still don't have words...just...thank you. All of you. I don't know what else to say." She blinked back the tears again.

"Don't just stand there. Play something." Charles waved a hand toward the piano.

Brenna moved the piano bench into place, arranged her skirt, and then held her hands poised over the keys, wanting to touch, but also wanting to savor the moment. Pressing her fingertips ever so lightly upon the keys, she ran through a menagerie of scales and chords, her confidence increasing and her ear tuned to the sounds.

"It's still well-tuned, even after the lengthy travel to get here."

"Good. Now, play some real music. Something we'll recognize." Charles prodded again.

"Let me look." Brenna shuffled through the sheet music, alternately considering and dismissing pieces, until she found the one she hoped she'd find. "Here it is!" She propped the music in front of her. "This is one of my favorites to hear and to play. Drew, without looking, do you remember what it is?"

He thought for a few seconds. "I do! Beethoven's Piano Sonata No. 14." His grin broadened.

"Yes. By what other name do we know it?"

"Moonlight Sonata."

"And which movement is it?"

"Well, the first, of course."

She laughed at his brotherly chastisement for her skepticism that he wouldn't know. With an apologetic, sweeping glance around the room, she said, "I haven't played in quite some time, so forgive me if I hit a few sour notes."

But her fingers remembered, and the melancholy notes wafted away on the prairie breeze.

***

The next day, Matt, James, and Charles rode out to check the water sources and the water gaps where the fences likely washed out from the rains while generally looking over the cattle and the condition of the grass they'd have to get through the winter. While the men were gone, Brenna busied herself with assisting in the settling in of the other households. Then, expecting the men home at the end of the third day and with the dogs as company, she strolled down the road. The sun on its downward journey behind the Spanish Peaks still offered ample light for her to see the riders returning home.

Home. Matt was coming home. On a contented sigh, her thoughts wandered back over the weeks since she'd found him half-drowned in the creek. Matt had fit into her life as if he'd always been with her on this ranch. He was as much a part of it as any of her family. She cherished the long, hot days of working together, their conversations over supper, watching the stars come out, then spending the rest of the night in each other's arms, and—

Realization hit her with a rush of surprise spreading like the warmth from a blazing fire from her head to her toes and out to the tips of her fingers. Could it be? Was it even possible? Did she dare hope?

Tell him. This one is strong. This child will live.

Somehow, she knew it was true. But the heartache of remembered disappointment and grief won out. Tilting her head toward the whisper at her ear, she said, "Not yet. It's too soon. Another month, to be sure." Keeping secrets wasn't in her nature, but this one she'd hold close to her heart for just a while longer.

Matt waved, and Brenna waved back as she stepped out to meet him on feet as light as her spirits.

***

With the first day of autumn came heightened expectation of the herd's arrival. When Matt couldn't find Brenna within the compound, he'd walk out to the south pasture where he'd find her sitting in the shade of trees clustered at the site of a spring with a book in hand and a clear view of the trail the herd would come down.

She greeted him with a smile today, and he sat on the ground beside her.

"You're going to stare a hole in the side of that hill."

Brenna giggled. "I'm just so eager for them to be here."

"I've been thinking about that. Let's ride out to meet them."

She gave him an odd look. "I'd not considered the possibility."

"We'll pack grub for a week and just head south. If we don't find them in a couple of days, we'll come back."

"When will we leave?"

"Pack tomorrow. Leave at first light the next day."

Brenna closed her book, nodding as she thought it over.

"Let's take Drew along."

Uncertainty crossed her brow. "He's never ridden farther than the small pasture on the old mare, and the milk cows frighten him. He climbed the fence and wouldn't come down when the rooster flapped his wings at him. He's afraid of the dark—"

Matt's raised eyebrows stopped her.

"Ohhh." It was a drawn out revelation, and a slow smile replaced her frown. "It's just what he needs, isn't it?"

Matt nodded.

"We'll have to ask my parents."

"I already did. They said he was old enough to decide on his own."

Brenna jumped to her feet and grabbed Matt's arm. "Let's ask him right now."

Drew's excitement for an adventure was as great as his fear of trying something new, but excitement won out, and at first light a day later, Brenna topped Trinchera Pass riding the roan filly, with Drew behind her on Samson, and Matt bringing up the rear, leading the two pack mules. They rode around the east side of the extinct Capulin volcano and headed across the open expanse of the northern New Mexico Territory on a southerly course that took them along the Goodnight-Loving trail.

South of Bueyeros, they crested a rise to the sight of four thousand head of cattle strung out over several miles. This wasn't Matt's first time to witness a herd on the trail, but it still struck him with awe that a couple of dozen cowboys could keep that many cattle moving together to a destination months beyond where they'd started. He'd taken his turn at riding herd, and he harbored a healthy respect for these men.

Drew tugged Matt's sleeve, pointing and smiling, almost bouncing in his seat.

"You look like you're about to bust wide open with questions. What do you want to know?"

"Everything."

Chuckling, Matt prompted, "Got to start somewhere. Ask."

"Where do the cowboys sleep?"

"On the ground in their bedrolls. Just like we've been doing since we left the ranch."

Drew made a face. "That's not very comfortable. What about when it rains and there's lightning? Or the wind blows? Or when it gets cold?"

"Same way. On the ground. There isn't any place else for them to sleep."

"So who watches the cattle at night when they're all asleep?"

"They ride night herd in shifts."

Drew shook his head, not understanding. "Shifts? What's that?"

"Taking turns every three or four hours. Once the cattle bed down for the night, a couple of cowboys ride clockwise and a couple more go counterclockwise around the perimeter of the herd, that way they can check in with each other as they meet and pass." Matt demonstrated with his hands. "They usually sing or talk quietly the whole time. Some recite poetry. The sound of their voices keeps the cattle calm."

Drew shook his head, frowning. "I wouldn't like to do that. Sounds scary. Coyotes and Indians are out there at night."

Matt chuckled. "Well, coyotes, but you don't have to worry about Indians. That's just in stories you've read. Most of the time, nothing exciting happens on a cattle drive. In fact, it can be downright boring."

"How do they eat? Do they make campfires like we did?" He took a drink from his canteen and wiped his mouth on his sleeve.

"The outfit has a cook and a helper who drive a chuck wagon and do all the cooking for the men. Generally, the cook makes three meals a day. The cowboys take turns watching the cattle and eating. But they all eat in a hurry. One of the most important things on a cattle drive is to have an experienced cook who knows how to fix a good meal fast then get the chuck wagon ahead of the herd to set up for the next camp. Every day on the trail costs money. Drives are slow enough without a cook hindering the daily progress, especially when you consider that, on a good day, the herd only covers ten or twelve miles."

Drew waved his arm, pointing across the prairie. "So why are the cattle all spread out? Won't they run off?"

"The cattle naturally spread out as they graze. The whole herd can't water at the same time, so the cowboys stagger groups of cattle to let the water holes have a chance to fill up for the next bunch."

Matt pointed. "Now, see how the cowboys are positioned on both sides of the herd?"

"Uh-huh."

"Those up front are riding point, then about a third of the way back are the swing riders. The cowboys near the end are riding flank. The ones following the herd are riding drag. They each have certain responsibilities to keep the herd going and together, and to round up strays and such." Matt pointed to the front of the herd. "Now, you see those few way out front? Well, those are lead cows. They set the pace for the herd."

"I'd like that job," Drew said, pointing at the horses.

"That's the *remuda*. The two riders taking care of them are the wranglers. It's their job for the entire drive."

Brenna stood in her stirrup. "Drew, look! Uncle Pete and Jim."

The two men galloped their horses up the gentle slope, their somber, somewhat suspicious expressions turning to wide grins when they recognized Brenna. Matt saw Jim shoot a quick glance in his direction, then back to Brenna, who nodded a response to some silent message that passed between them.

Pete said, "I thought you might come looking for us. It's good to see you, Brenna." He looked at Matt, then at Drew. "And who are these fellows?"

"This is your nephew, Drew."

Pete's face showed his surprise. "Last time I saw you, you were still wearing short pants. Glad to meet you again."

Jim slapped Drew on the back. "Hey, little brother. You're just about man-grown."

Matt didn't wait for Brenna to introduce him. He held out his hand to Pete. "Matt Caddock."

Pete spit a long brown line of tobacco juice into an ant hill as he grasped Matt's hand. "I know you from the Clifton House hold-up some years back. Saved a few lives that day, you did. You've got yourself a name as a bad man with a gun."

"Yes, sir. And I've worked hard to earn it. Nurtured it until it was full grown and old enough to take care of itself, then I turned it loose on about anything that got in my way."

At the edge of his vision, Matt saw Brenna turn a sharp look. Pete squinted, spat again, and burst out with a deep, hearty laugh. "You'll do, Caddock. I like your sense of humor." Pete sent an eyebrow-raised question to Brenna. "How'd you and Drew hook up with such a tough *hombre*?"

"Oh, he rode in on a storm one day and hasn't been in a hurry to leave."

Pete's nod said he didn't need to know more. Matt swung his gaze to Brenna's brother to face the scrutiny he'd been under since he'd ridden up, and he met the same sparkling blue eyes he'd come to know in Brenna. The twin resemblance was strong.

"Well, Matt, it's about time you showed up. What the hell took you so long?" A friendly, sideways grin of greeting spread over his face.

Matt pushed his hat back. "I guess I just kept taking the wrong fork in the trail."

"Are you on the right trail now?"

Matt took the insinuation for what it was—a brother's concern about Matt's intentions toward his sister. He answered honestly. "It's a second chance trail for me, and I aim to stay on it clear to the end."

Jim nodded. "That's all any of us can hope for. Welcome to the family. Know anything about cattle?"

"I followed a herd up the Chisholm Trail a few years ago."

Jim reined his horse around. "We could use some extra wranglers."

Brenna and Drew fell in with Jim and Pete, but Matt remained where he was, watching and thinking. It was good, being accepted into Brenna's family. So good that it was easy to ignore the threat of Archer looking for him. When he gave Socks his head to follow, a shiver skittered down Matt's spine. He'd heard it said when that happened out of the blue, someone had just walked where your grave would be. Damn those old wives tales, messing with a man's mind.

Chapter Twelve

The first Saturday evening in October brought about a supper celebration for James and Ann's anniversary. Ranch hands and family gathered around the summer table for a hearty meal, after which conversation turned to cattle and plans for the future. Matt rested his crossed arms on the edge of the table and listened to the talk while nursing along a cup of coffee.

Pete commented. "The open range is vanishing. I saw it coming ten years ago. We encountered fenced land all the way up from Texas."

Jim said, "We're part of that vanishing. We fenced our land, and so did our neighbors. Dara's family fenced before we did. And I've talked to some farmers up on Johnson Mesa."

"Asa Everett has a good reason for fencing. He's breeding a line of quarter horses that are selling for a pretty penny. He can't just turn them out to forage and make it on their own." Pete held up his coffee cup for Aggie to top it off as she walked by.

Jim paused to look up and down the table. "I think it's time to tear down the compound walls. They've served us well, but their usefulness is past. We close the gates at night out of habit, not because we need the protection. The turn of the century is just around the corner. It would behoove us to move forward with it."

James asked, "Do you have suggestions?"

Jim nodded. "I do. We could plat-out a town and sell lots. I think people would come in from all over in no time. We'd have a school and a church, maybe even a post office. There's talk of bringing electricity and telephone lines into Trinidad. It's not that much of a stretch to get it on out here. We could get enough folks to put down roots here, we'd have some leverage to get a railroad spur. We've got the best water source in twenty miles or more right in the middle of the compound."

"That's the way of it now. Progress and civilization." Pete grunted a humorless what-can-you-do-about-it laugh. "Can't stop it, so we might as well learn to live with it."

James spoke up. "Jim, your ideas are excellent. We'll pursue this further as time allows. As far as our collective future is concerned, we've got land enough to support two years' worth of calves, but any longer, and we'll run into overgrazing."

"Yeah, that many head will push the grass dangerously short," Jim confirmed. "Better count on mild winters, wet springs, not-too-hot summers, and late frost in the fall." Jim shook his head. "But anyone who thinks for a minute that the weather'll cooperate when we need it most is a fool or a greenhorn, and I've never noticed much difference between the two.

"Many of us right here remember we had two hard winters in a row. The first one came in on the shirttails of a dry spring and summer, which made it all the worse for ranchers running cattle who hadn't put-by enough winter feed. Then, the very next year, blizzards hit up north harder than here. We got by all right that winter."

Nods and murmurs moved in and among the year-round ranch hands.

Pete added, "That's where we're different from most folks. We prepare for the worst of times and count our blessings when it passes us over. We've got plenty of winter feed stored up. As long as we can break a trail to the cattle, we can get the hay wagons to them." He looked up and down the length of the table. "Luck was smiling on this family that you were behind in your plans on moving back. November on through the late spring thaw, we just had some riding stock and a few cows right close to take care of. Even then, it was all me and Aggie, Jim, Charles, and Mary and our regular hands could take care of. I've seen a lot of winters, but nothing like the snow we had then. *Mmm mmm mmm.*" He shook his head. "Those were some hard months."

Jim concurred. "Even with feed stockpiled, we'd have lost most of the herd that winter and probably had to sell out before the next winter just to pay bills. Ranchers all the way into Montana and the Dakotas went bankrupt because of those two hard years."

James interjected, "Our finances are solid enough that until the cattle are sold, barring catastrophic events, we have enough for all of us to live on without scrimping, as well as cover the ranch expenses, including paying the hired hands." James turned his gaze to Matt. "If our venture doesn't pay off in beef, then we will chalk this up to an expensive adventure and return east."

Pete chimed in, "The beef market went to hell after those two cattle-killing winters. It'll take some time for it to swing back up. If we can hold out selling until then, we'll do all right."

The table conversation went on without him as Matt drifted off into thoughts he seldom acknowledged. He was part of what was vanishing from the West. The days of the hired gun were all but over. Like Pete, he'd seen it coming for some time. He admired the Stirling clan for their high hopes and indomitable perseverance to carve a future from the land for the coming generations. But putting all their assets into a venture that depended upon the favorable whims of nature with faith that, given time, a bottomed-out cattle market would turn a profit, seemed like a sure-fire recipe for ruin. Buying ocean-side property in the Arizona Territory held better prospects than what they faced.

When Brenna brought another pot of coffee around, Drew begged her, "Play the piano for us, Brenna, please."

She refilled Matt's cup. "What do you want to hear?"

"That loud music. You know, the *dah, dah, dah, dahhhhhh.*"

Brenna laughed. "That is a Beethoven symphony, not piano music for such a quiet, beautiful evening."

"Well, then, you choose something."

Brenna left the coffee pot on the table, gave Matt's shoulder a light squeeze as she passed him, and took Drew's hand.

"I know the perfect piece. Brahms' cradle song."

A few minutes later, music graced the night air. Matt had never heard it, but she'd chosen well. The lullaby cadence added a serene feel to the already peaceful evening. The men went on talking, but restlessness worked its way into Matt's mind, and he excused himself to be alone.

Ann intercepted him. "Do you mind if I join you for a stroll?"

"I don't mind at all. I'm going to close-up the barn and the gates."

"It is a lovely evening for a walk under the stars."

Matt glanced up, nodding. "Yes, ma'am, it is."

Whatever was on her mind, she was in no hurry to share, so Matt lingered at the corral with Socks where he hung his head over the corral rail for Matt to rub his ears. Silent minutes dragged by, and Matt decided he needed to help her along, or they'd be out here all night.

"Ma'am, I have a feeling you want to say something. Go ahead and say it straight out."

She turned her back to the corral rails. "Please, you must call me Ann."

Matt nodded. "Yes, ma'am."

With a head-shaking grin of acceptance that he wasn't going to do that any time soon, she said, "Matt, Brenna loves you, and you've proven you feel the same for her. But I wonder if you realize the depth of her love."

"If you want to know why I haven't married her... Well, she more or less told me no when I asked her. I understand how you might question my intentions."

Ann cut him off with a wave and a tsking tongue-click. "No. There is no question of your devotion. James and I already think of you as our son."

"But?"

"Do you know why we left here when Brenna and Jim were young?"

"Brenna said it was too dangerous to stay with the Indian raiding."

"A simplistic, but accurate statement. The precipitant to our move was a war party that attacked the compound. I was wounded, and Jim was taken."

Matt's eyebrows shot up. "Taken as in kidnapped?"

"Yes. James, Pete, and Charles followed the warriors. Without belaboring the details, and though it took many days, they brought Jim back unharmed. We left here not long after."

Matt didn't interrupt the silence of her faraway thoughts. In her own good time, she continued.

"There is something you must know about Brenna and me." She glanced toward the summer table then to Brenna's house before she looked back at Matt. "Neither of us could ever live where our men aren't. This is the second time I've left Philadelphia to accompany James here. I met James when he came to Philadelphia as an apprentice, of sorts. James and Pete had interests and skills in wood-working. Charles wanted them to train under a master, so Charles arranged for the brothers to learn from a friend in Philadelphia. Pete returned first, then James followed a year or so later."

"And you came back with him."

"Yes. I am the oldest daughter of that Philadelphia friend." Ann smiled at revealing her little secret. "You see, it doesn't matter to me where we live, as long as James and I are together. Brenna is the same. She will accompany you no matter where you go, regardless of the hardship, and she will never regret her decision. All she wants is to be where you are."

"I know what this place means to her. I'd never ask her to leave." Matt shifted his weight, trying to wrap his thoughts around words that would reassure Ann of his intentions. "I've been wandering since I was a kid. I lost my parents early on and a few years later, the man who raised me died. I think of having a home and a family. And if I was lucky enough to have them... Well, it's not something I take lightly. I'd not throw them away."

Ann nodded as she studied him. "Yes, I believe you would do everything within your power to take care of them."

"If you don't mind my asking, Brenna told me you and Mr. Stirling—"

"First names," Ann chided.

Matt shifted his weight again, not finding it any easier to call Brenna's father by his first name than it was to do the same with Ann, so he avoided it. "Why did you two wait so long to get married?"

"James simply wasn't ready, and I understood that. I had to know he didn't need to ride beyond the horizon or over another mountain pass just to see the other side. He has an adventurous spirit, which is why we've come back here. He made the best of our years in Philadelphia, even though his heart remained here. At the time, it was the right decision to raise our family in the east. We don't regret that decision, because we knew we'd eventually return. As for why we married when we did." Her smile was as warm as her soft, wistful sigh. "It was time. It was simply time."

Brenna had spoken those same words.

"So you think I still have trails to ride and mountains to cross?"

"I watched you while the talk went on about the cattle and the ranch. You listened, but in your thoughts, you traveled a lone road. I recognized the look in your eyes. James often has those same yearnings. I know what it means."

"You're right. There is a road I'm going to travel. Have to travel."

It was uncanny how Ann and Brenna knew what was inside his head and his heart better than he did.

"She'll understand whatever it is you must do, but don't lie to her. She will forgive anything but that."

"The road I'm going on leads back here. And here is where I'm going to stay."

"I hope so, Matt. I certainly hope so. For your sake, as much as Brenna's"

There was truth in her words, for he knew high hopes and sincere intentions weren't enough to overcome the challenges life tended to throw out when a person least expected.

***

Matt stayed on the porch well into the night, just standing in the doorway with a shoulder leaning against the doorjamb and his thoughts far away to the west. A match strike, then the wavering shadows of lamp light from the kitchen, preceded the door opening and closing behind him.

"Are you looking for the next trail?"

There was no accusation in her voice.

"It's been on my mind tonight."

"I have no hold on you."

He nodded.

"You're going after the gold, aren't you?"

He faced her. "Yes."

"I suspected as much. I saw it in your eyes when the talk turned to cattle and finances tonight. You're concerned about our solvency, aren't you?"

So much like her mother in observation and intuition.

"This ranch and your family mean everything to me. I don't want to see it fail before it has a chance to begin."

"From the moment you told me about the gold, I knew you'd search for it someday. You just had to have the right reason."

"Then, you know me better than I know myself. Until tonight, I never intended to look for it. I can't come into this family empty-handed, Brenna. As a man, I've got to pull my own weight. Right now, I'm just a drifter, a gunfighter with nothing to show in my life but a reputation I'm not so proud of anymore. Your husband was a partner in the ranch, and you should expect no less of me. You should know those are some big shoes to fill."

"You've proven yourself to my family. They know you as a hard-working man of your word. You've shown them integrity and devotion to the ranch and to me. They don't need more than that to know your worth as a man. And neither do I. The gold means nothing to me, and they don't know about it."

He looked at her a long time to remember this moment—hands clutching the front of her shawl, her hair hanging loose, and her eyes soft and sorrowful with the knowledge of his leaving.

"Best keep it that way until after I'm gone. They'll want to talk me out of it."

She remained silent as he walked to her.

"I realized tonight what it meant to Henry for me to get his gold. I owe it to him to honor his dying wishes. I finally understand what he meant when he told me to do something good with the gold and find me a good woman." He took hold of her hands. "You know I have to do this."

"When are you leaving?"

"At daylight."

"I won't stand in your way, but I don't have to like it."

"Gold or not, I'll come back." Wrapping his arms around her, he rested his chin on the crown of her head, and stroked her hair where it lay long and silky down her back, shimmering with a bronze-red sheen under the soft light from the kitchen. "If I don't, you'll know I'm dead."

She shook her head against his chest. "You'll be back. Gregory promised, and he was a man of his word, too. I want you to take Samson. He's stout and sensible. I'll feel as if a part of me is riding with you, and with Socks here, he'll be my reminder that you're coming back."

"I've got something for you." Matt dug into a front pocket of his trousers and withdrew a bit of faded cloth that he unfolded and held flat on his palm. Light shimmered on a gold heart strung on a tarnished gold chain necklace. "It's all I have left to remind me of my mother. Pa had it in his hand when he died."

Long years and many miles lay between him and those memories, but he still blinked back the sting of losing his parents. When Brenna raised her gaze from the necklace, her eyes shone with tears that spoke silently of how much this meant to her. She held her hair up while he hooked the clasp at the back of her neck. Glancing down, she smiled and touched the heart where it lay upon her chest.

"I was going to give it to you in the morning, but it's more fitting now. Wear it to keep me close to you just like it kept my mother close to my pa."

"I will. Now, come to bed. Daylight is hours away. Let's not spend them out here."

***

Dense fog lay upon the land as if nature itself acknowledged the somber morning. Brenna rode at Matt's side to the foot of the Trinchera Pass trail where he'd begin his lone journey. Matt turned Samson so he faced Brenna with his knee pressed up to hers. Her eyes, as blue as he'd ever seen them, held no tears, only determination to endure what a woman must. When he touched the little gold heart, she grasped his hand and held it to her chest.

"I'm coming back."

"Those words come from your heart, but neither of us is naïve. Gold changes a man. It can make him forget where he's heading."

"It can remind him what he's returning to, just as well."

"Then only time and fate will know the outcome." She set her shoulders and lifted her chin. "You come home, Matt Caddock."

His insides crumbled at the hope she forced through the tears in her voice. Swallowing hard, he said, "When I do, we'll make this permanent."

"Then you'd better have a preacher with you."

"Get yourself a new dress. I'm partial to yellow." He managed a grin despite the heaviness of parting in his heart. "Reminds me of the day we met. And yellow makes those big blue eyes of yours shine like sunlight on prairie flowers."

She hung her head, smiling, but he saw the hasty wipe she made at her eyes. Lord, how he wanted to kiss her, hold her in his arms one more time, but if he did, it would make the inevitable good-bye even harder. So, he traded one regret for another, and backed Samson away until their joined hands became outstretched arms, and finally only fingertips touching.

"I'll be back before the first snow falls on your stone paths."

Then that fragile bond between their fingertips broke when he turned Samson's head up the trail. Until he'd met Brenna, Matt had never looked back, but now he wanted to see what leaving looked like. He turned in the saddle to watch her as she became a faint shape and then nothing more than memory as the fog closed around her. Then a flittering breeze disturbed the air, clearing the space between them for an instant, and Matt could have sworn he saw Gregory walking down the path behind her.

Chapter Thirteen

Matt Caddock was a man with a simple plan—find the gold and return to Brenna by the first snow at the ranch. He didn't have much time. No more than a month, if that. Too bad simple plans weren't necessarily the easiest.

Riding under a promise of a cool evening, his arrival in Taos turned no heads. He was just a stranger going somewhere, but headed nowhere. Skirting the edge of the quiet adobe town, he circled wide around the ruins of the old San Geronimo Church and graveyards until he reached the back of the *Nuestra Señora de Guadalupe* parish.

Looping the horse's reins around a short post, he gave him a pat and a promise he'd return soon, then he walked along the adobe wall to the courtyard gate, his gaze scanning the street, buildings, and passersby.

At the church door, he paused, glanced around, then stepped into the cool tranquility inside the church and removed his hat. He lingered at the side of the doorway, letting his eyes adjust to the change in light while getting his bearings. The floor fell away in a gentle slope to the front where candles burned and a shadowed cross hung high on the far wall.

Movement, and a barely audible scraping—like a footstep—caught his ear, and he expected a priest or a parishioner to greet him...but no one appeared. Chalking it up to a mouse scurrying about, Matt walked up the narrow aisle to the first pew where he'd sat beside Henry on that long ago day in his seventeen-year-old life. He took the same place on the wooden pew where he'd sat with Henry, and gazed at the serene white figure of the Lady of Guadalupe nestled into her protective alcove carved into the two-foot-thick adobe wall not five feet in front of him.

He had dim recollections of going to church a couple of times a year with his parents, but never again after his ma died. The only other time he'd been in a church was with Henry here.

He was uncomfortable in a church, because he didn't know what to do. When he'd voiced his misgivings, Henry had explained a church was a place to think. You didn't have to pray if you didn't want to. So that's what he'd done. He'd thought.

He'd wondered about his future as much as he questioned why his parents had died and left him a penniless orphan. There seemed no point to anything in his life with the aimless drifting from job-to-job and town-to-town with Henry. Together, all they owned was a pocket full of nothing. Granted, they had clothes on their backs and food in their bellies, but wasn't there more out there...somewhere?

Guilt stinging his conscience for those ungrateful thoughts, he'd peeked at Henry. His eyes were closed and his chin rested on his chest. It was the first time Matt had looked at Henry. Really looked.

He had to be pushing seventy. Too old to be traipsing the country. He should be sitting on a front porch somewhere drinking lemonade and watching the clouds pass by.

Realization hit him that they'd traded places. He couldn't pin down when it happened, but he'd become more of a caretaker to Henry than Henry was to him. It wasn't Henry keeping them on the move. He, Matt, had the wanderlust, and Henry was content to tag along.

That's when he knew it was up to him to see Henry through however many years he had left. That was his future, at least for a while longer. But then what? The thought of Henry dying left Matt with a cold, empty feeling deep inside. Without Henry, he had no one. When that happened, what purpose would he have for living?

Now, years after Henry's death, Matt had found purpose, but if he knew nothing else about life, he knew everything came with a price. Could he have Brenna and the gold without paying with his soul? It was too late to worry about that. Much as he loved Brenna, he'd made promises to Henry, and it was time to come good for his word.

Head hanging, Matt closed his eyes. *I'm here, Henry. Show me where you hid the letter.* Opening his eyes, he considered where he would have hidden a letter to keep it undisturbed through the years. The logical place was with the Lady herself.

Careful to keep a firm grasp so she didn't slip through his hands, he lifted the statue and turned it every which way. It was just a carved two-foot-tall white wooden statue, solid and simple. With special care, he placed the Lady on the floor, then ran his hands along the inside of her alcove sanctuary, hoping for a secret door. But rapping his knuckles on the sides told him the walls were as solid as the Lady herself.

Replacing the statue, he squatted on his heels to get a different view.

He sensed, more than saw, movement near the church door at the same time a slight grating sound reached him. His hands moved toward his guns as he pivoted on the ball of a foot, searching for the source of the noise. Uneasiness crawled down his spine that despite hearing noises and seeing movement, he was still alone. Maybe it was his conscience warning that anyone watching would think he was stealing or vandalizing. Explaining he was looking for clues to a hidden cache of gold wouldn't be much help to convince anyone otherwise.

Brushing off his jumpiness, he blew out a long, slow breath and tipped his head back. Overhead, a thick, heavy timber ceiling cross-beam ran the width of the church and ended in the adobe wall and right over the Lady's alcove. As he studied the beam, he noticed a space of a few inches between the beam and ceiling. A niggling idea took shape.

Dragging the end of the pew to stand on, Matt stepped up and ran his hand across the top of the beam right above the statue. His fingertips touched a solid object, but it was too far back to grasp. Balancing on his toes and using one hand to brace himself, he stretched his other arm farther into the narrow space and managed to catch an edge with a fingernail and drag it forward enough to wrap his fingers around it. Whatever was inside had some weight.

Stepping down, he pushed the pew back into place, sat, and inspected what he'd found.

A handkerchief box. His ma had one something like it that she'd kept on her chest of drawers. This box was the shape and design of a miniature traveling trunk with a hinged lid, five or six inches long, four inches wide, and a couple of inches deep, with wear on the corners. Slipping the clasp, he lifted the lid.

He didn't find handkerchiefs, and he didn't expect to. Tucked side-by-side upon the faded red satin interior, two rolled papers the length of the box lay behind two muslin drawstring tobacco pouches, one at each end. Nestled in the center was a gold nugget the size of a Robin's egg.

Picking up the nugget, he turned it every which way, marveling at its size and rich color. It was the biggest piece of gold he'd ever seen. With the box balanced across his knees, he put the nugget back, opened one of the drawstring pouches, and shook out the contents. Twenty shiny Double Eagles. The other pouch held the same. Placing the box beside him, he took out the smaller paper, saw it was a map, and set it aside. Unrolling the other paper, he smoothed it out on the top of his thigh, spreading his fingers to keep it from curling up. Right off, he recognized Henry's rough scrawl. As he read, Matt heard Henry's voice in the words.

Matt

Yer readin this cause I'm gone and yer goin after the gold. You need to know how I come by the gold aint somethin I'm proud of and I'll go to hell for it sure as shootin. Me and my saddle pardner Clem Johnson found the gold on Baldy Mountain back in '41 more than 25 years before the rush.

It was the durndest thing I ever did see. Nuggets like rocks was a layin on the ground for a man to just reach down and pick up. We even panned more gold right out of the stream. 'Twarnt no diggin. I tell you Matt it was a mother lode.

We just bagged up what we could carry out on three pack mules and lit off that mountain in a snow. We marked a tree so we could find the spot again come spring but I never did go back.

We got down that mountain to Cimarron. It was a spit of a town on the Santa Fe Trail back then. We swore not to tell a livin soul. But we got mighty drunk celebratin and the short of it is Clem got to runnin his mouth and I killed him to shut him up. I hightailed it out of there ahead of a lynchin.

I made it as far as the Mexican Mountains when my ridin horse and mules bout give out from the run I'd made through the Sangres. So I filled my pockets with nuggets and dropped that gold in a hole and scratched out a map.

Five years runnin I went back. I was mindful where I showed those nuggets so folks wouldn't get to wonderin where it come from but that's just what happened. I had to stop for a good long while. I feared someone would follow and take the gold.

The last time I took enough to last us a while if we was careful and I swung down to Taos and left you this letter and the map in the box. You might like to know I was borned and raised in Taos and I come to this church ever Sunday til I lit out on my own after my folks died when I was fifteen.

You was the closest I had to a son and there was never one better nor one who could of made me prouder so I'm tellin you that you got to do better with your life than I did.

I killed Clem out of greed. Pure mean greed. He was the only man I ever called friend until you come along. There was a time I had me a good woman but it warnt til after she died that I knowed I'd lost somethin I'd never have again. I miss that woman. I sorely do.

The only regret I have in this world is that I didn't love her like she deserved and she shore as hell deserved more than an old saddle bum the likes of me. Matt there aint nothin closer to heaven than the love of a good woman. And there aint nothin else will save a man's soul from hell. Not prayin. Not confession. Only a woman's love. Find you a good woman and treat her right.

I give you them double eagles cause you need to buy an outfit then git yerself to the north side of the Mexican Mountains to where we set up camp and fished and hunted that spring when you was a youngster and then again in the summer when you was older. Take the way we went so it looks right when you git there. Never forget findin the gold aint the hard part. Doin right by it is.

Henry

Matt swiped the back of his hand across his eyes. In all his years with Henry, he'd never known anything of a personal nature about him. Maybe Henry had dropped hints, maybe he hadn't, either way, Matt was ashamed he didn't recall or hadn't paid attention. He'd been too wrapped up in his own kid-thoughts to be interested in what Henry held in his heart.

Damn, he missed that old man.

Rerolling the letter, he returned both papers to the box, closed the lid, and wedged it between his gun belt and waist of his trousers. With another look at the Lady, he thanked her for keeping Henry's secret safe, put his hat on, and headed toward the door.

At the last pew, he turned for one last look. A beam of sunset light illuminated the Lady's alcove, and she glowed with a warm white radiance. With a nod of goodbye, he opened the door.

A shadow of movement crossed the threshold, and he ran head-long into an invisible wall. Staggering backward, his mind didn't comprehend what he couldn't see. He stepped forward again, and the same thing happened. The doorway was clear, yet not clear. A sheer, milky veil hung in the air between him and the outside world.

"What the hell?" he muttered.

Ducking his chin, he bulled his way through the doorway. The harder he pushed, the firmer the invisible wall became two points of pressure on his chest, as if hands held him back. His skin crawled; a chill gripped him. Rational thought left him. Swinging punches at his shadowy assailant, he flailed at the air, realizing he looked a fool fighting with nothing, but that didn't stop him.

The sight of the man on the big raw-boned sorrel paint did. There was only one man he knew who rode a horse of that size and color.

Archer.

Riding with him were three men Matt knew all too well. Herker, Walt, and that damned crazy Vernon.

Shit.

Matt didn't breathe. He didn't blink. Archer glanced into the churchyard, his gaze lingering on the opened church door. Matt knew Archer was too far away to make out anything inside the dark church, but he was close enough that Matt heard the conversation with the group of men going by. Their exchange was in Mexican, but Matt followed it without trouble.

Archer told the men he was looking for his friend, Matt Caddock, who rode a bay gelding with four white socks and a blaze face. After some discussion, the men concurred they didn't know Matt, but one man suggested Archer ask at the cantina in the plaza.

Matt listened to the receding hoof beats. It was just a matter of asking until Archer found someone who knew he was living at the Stirling Compound. The search for the gold suddenly became a race to get back to Brenna before Archer paid her a visit.

With a tentative step forward, one hand hovering above his gun and his other arm outstretched to feel his way, Matt expected to hit the invisible wall, but the way was clear. Whatever had been there was gone.

He stepped into the sunshine, breathing in the hot dusty aroma of the hard-packed dirt street. It was time to get out of town. Fast. Matt went around to the back of the church to Samson and took his time checking the cinch while looking around to make sure Archer wasn't anywhere in sight. The only person nearby was a man standing between two crumbling adobe buildings. Matt dismissed him as no one of concern—then, recognition hit him. He jerked his gaze back just as the man disappeared between the two old buildings.

"I'll be damned. He kept me from walking right out into Archer." Matt patted Samson on the shoulder. "Be right back, boy."

On a jog-trot, Matt followed Gregory. When he burst from between buildings, Matt bowled into a man, and his only thought was he'd finally caught this ghostly prowler. Matt grabbed the man by the front of his coat and pushed him against a wall.

"Why are you following me?"

For many seconds, Matt couldn't grasp that this slight-built, blond-haired young man with his spectacles askew didn't look at all like Gregory. He wore a dark, store-bought frock coat that had seen better days, a white shirt with a black, folded string tie, and a flat-crowned farmer hat. Then he saw the book on the ground and put it together. Releasing the man, Matt stepped back, sweeping his gaze far to near and into every nook and cranny for Gregory.

"Sorry, Parson. I mistook you for someone else." Matt picked up the Bible, brushed it off, and handed it to the young man.

The man straightened his spectacles. "Don't trouble yourself. It was my fault for not announcing my passing as I crossed between abandoned buildings in broad daylight."

Matt rubbed a hand across the back of his neck, accepting the sarcasm and gentle chastisement in the preacher's words. He also saw a glint of amusement and an abundance of kindness in his eyes.

"I'm John Clement. Reverend John Joseph Clement." He held out his hand.

The man's hand hung in the air, but Matt only heard Brenna's voice. *You'd better have a preacher with you.*

"Excuse me. You are..."

Matt grinned and took hold of John's hand. "Matt Caddock. Are you a preacher here?"

"No. I'm on a pilgrimage of sorts, traveling town-to-town until I receive direction for the way I'm to go."

"So you're a circuit rider."

"Actually, no. My hope is to find a place to settle where I can build a church."

Nodding, and with a plan taking shape, Matt asked, "Did you see a man come through here—two, maybe three minutes ago? He's not as tall as me, with light brown hair and wearing dark clothes like a new suit, but no hat?"

"In fact, I did. He was some yards ahead of me and appeared to need assistance. As I hurried to help him, I ran into you. I'm afraid I didn't see which way he went."

Matt shook his head, the grin on his face widening. "Doesn't matter. I have a feeling he'll show up again." He threw his arm across John's shoulders and guided him along toward Samson. "You ever hunt for buried treasure, Parson?"

Chapter Fourteen

Dogs barking brought Brenna to her kitchen door. Four men, strangers, rode into the compound and stopped in the yard. James greeted them and continued on with the end of his evening stroll that would take him in front of her house on the way to his. Pete talked at length to the man riding a strikingly colored sorrel paint gelding while pointing toward the summer table then he accompanied the group to the barn to help them put up their horses and give them hay and grain, as was their habit when travelers stopped in. After a few minutes, Pete went to his house for supper.

The paint horse seemed familiar, but she couldn't remember why. She was sure she'd never seen the rider or the horse before. The rider of the paint horse left the barn ahead of his companions and walked toward the summer table with much more interest in looking the place over and in petting the dogs than Brenna thought necessary. Something in his manner and bearing made her uncomfortable. Then, it came to her.

Archer.

Her breath caught, and her gaze went straight to his holsters. Two guns with the grips positioned backward, just like Matt had explained. Her heart leaped into her throat. She'd neglected to warn her family about Archer, and she regretted that oversight. With a deep breath to bolster her nerve, she took up her shotgun and walked out to greet Archer.

"Good evening. If you're staying the night, you're welcomed to stay in the bunkhouse with our hired men. You'll find plenty of spare beds. I can offer you coffee, cold meat, fresh bread, and pie."

"Thank you, ma'am," Archer said with a nod and touch to the brim of his hat. "Supper and a place to sleep is appreciated. We'll be on our way come daylight."

She forced a calm, confident front. "I'll be right out with coffee. Then I'll need a few minutes to prepare supper." When she turned, Archer's voice stopped her.

"You haven't asked my name. Makes me wonder if you don't already know who I am. Maybe...you were expecting me. Maybe someone warned you."

Brenna set her shoulders and faced him. Shotgun cradled in the crook of her arm, it was a natural move to tilt the double barrels up so they pointed in the general area of his gun belt buckle. She thought he almost smiled, and she was sure she saw a flicker of respect cross his eyes.

"Who you are is none of my business. This is a land in which a man can take any name he chooses, and there is no one to doubt him." Brenna looked straight at him. "Conversely, you haven't asked *my* name. It makes me wonder if you don't already know who *I* am. Perhaps you've been planning to stop in."

Now, he smiled. "Maybe I have. I heard you make bear sign on Sunday."

"You've heard correctly. I'll wrap some in a flour sack for you to take when you leave in the morning." With that, she went to her house, but she felt his gaze on her back like a hot poker ready to plunge between her shoulder blades.

James intercepted her. "Do you need help with supper for them?"

"No, but do you have a moment to talk?"

"Certainly. Is something wrong?"

"Possibly."

James followed her into the house, and explained as she worked. "Those men are not simply passing through. Matt used to ride with the leader. He goes by the name Archer. Matt expected Archer to come here looking for him. I don't know the others." She filled James in on the details and confessed about Matt's true reason for leaving.

James arched an eyebrow. "Gold? That's a generous undertaking on our behalf."

Brenna nodded. "It's important to him."

"And these men want that gold." James cast a glance toward the summer table. "This doesn't bode well."

"Since Matt isn't here, I'm hopeful they'll not return." She stepped to the door to check on the men. Drew came into the yard from outside the gates, which was curious, considering his trepidation of what lay beyond the walls out in the wide open prairie. It also seemed he was hurrying a little too fast for his usual dawdling manner. When Archer called him over, Drew cut a nervous glance toward her house before he veered from his path and went to the table.

"We mustn't appear nervous about their presence. So, you take the pot and cups out to them and converse as if they're the usual drifters passing through while also assuring them I'm preparing food. Then, as casually as you can, take Drew home. Without being obvious, get word to everyone else about this and have them stay inside. Warn them to be on the ready to deal with whatever arises. I don't know whether it's fortunate or lamentable that Jim and half of our hands are out on the range."

James nodded that he understood her concern. "All of our hired men are loyal. We can trust them to remain tight-lipped to questions. Archer won't have an easy time extracting information from of them—if that is, indeed, what he intends."

Brenna handed him four cups to put into the basket.

"What are you going to do?"

"Right now, I'll put supper together and take it to them." She handed him the coffee pot. "And then, I'll sit up all night with my shotgun on my lap."

James smiled. "That is my plan, as well. In the meantime, I'll watch from my house."

Brenna stayed at the kitchen door until James and Drew were safely home, then she prepared supper, and put it along with plates and tableware into two wicker baskets. Unwilling to face the men unarmed, but unable to carry her shotgun and two baskets, she went to her bedroom for her blunt-nosed .22 Reid knuckleduster in her bureau drawer.

Checking the seven loads, she tucked the small gun into the pocket she wore tied around her waist and concealed under her skirt. She practiced slipping her hand into the slit in the seam of her skirt to grasp the little gun, although she had no intention to withdraw it to pull the trigger. She'd shoot through the material.

The gun was only effective at close-range, and she had a feeling if she needed it at all, it would be face-to-face with a target she couldn't miss.

Lingering while the men filled their plates, Brenna said, "I'll bring out the pie, and another pot of coffee as soon as it's brewed."

"Thank you, ma'am," Archer said. "I'm curious about something."

Brenna waited for him to continue.

"Where's Matt Caddock? That's his blaze-faced bay with the white socks in the corral."

Prepared for just this inquiry, she did not lie. "Gone. He was here one day and on the trail the next."

"Why is his horse still here?"

"He traded for one of ours." Peripherally, she saw the slovenly, barrel-chested man leering at her with a gaze that traveled the length of her body like the crawling feet of a centipede. There was something off, something out-of-kilter in his eyes, and it frightened her in a way she'd never known.

"Did he say where he was going?"

Forcing down her revulsion, she waved a hand toward the prairie beyond the compound walls. "Where do drifters go? Somewhere out there. Now, excuse me."

Although Archer said nothing, she read the suspicion in his eyes. Gathering a handful of skirt, she returned to the house, and collapsed on a kitchen chair, her legs weak, and her hands trembling. These situations reminded her how much she wanted a window put in over the sink where she could observe the yard from a less noticeable position than standing at the kitchen door. Granted, the porch offered some concealment, but at the window, her movements wouldn't be as easily detected.

The sound of a footstep behind her brought her to her feet as she twirled to face the intruder with her hand reaching into the folds of her skirt for the gun.

"Brenna," Drew whispered, his head barely poking out from the bedroom doorway.

"Drew! Don't sneak up on me like that. How did you get in here?" A cold rush of relief steeped in fear that she might have shot him washed over her, and she brushed a shaking hand over her brow.

"I came around back of the houses to the side door at the bedroom. It wasn't locked."

"Why are you here?"

"I'm worried about you being alone without Matt." He hurried the few steps across the kitchen and hugged her around the waist.

"Thank you. I'll be all right." Standing back, she looked at him. "Now, why are you really here?"

"Matt's been gone a long time. Is he coming back?"

"Yes. Do you remember what he told you the morning he left?"

Drew nodded. "He promised to be back by the first snowfall."

"That's right. We have no reason to doubt him."

"But those men are after him."

Brenna turned from him to hide her alarm and busied herself with taking a peach pie from the pie safe and cutting it into quarters. "Why do you think that?"

"I was in the barn when they came in. I didn't like their looks, so I hid in the chicken house. They talked about recognizing Matt's horse. The man Archer said he was sure it was true what he'd heard in Cimarron about Matt taking up with a handsome widow lady out east of Trinidad. He laughed and said he'd get Matt's gold even if he had to wait here until he comes back with it. When they all left the barn, I slipped out the back and came around to the gates so they wouldn't know I was eavesdropping, but Archer called me over before I could warn you."

"What did he want?"

"He wanted to know how many people lived here."

"How did you respond?"

"I said there were dozens of people around any time day or night."

Brenna smiled. A useless, albeit well-intended lie. "Good for you."

"What did he mean about taking Matt's gold? Matt said the reason he was leaving was because he had business to take care of."

Brenna checked the coffee, decided it needed a few more minutes. "It is business. An old friend left him gold nuggets when he died, and Matt went to claim his inheritance." It was as simple an explanation as he needed right then.

"Oh, I understand that, but I sure wish Matt was here. He'd just shoot them. Then, it would be over. They'd all be dead, and we'd be safe."

Brenna opened her mouth to scold him, but stopped at the sight of the terrible fear shining in his eyes. Taking his hands in hers, she had to give him something safe, something hopeful he could hold on to.

"Drew, Matt isn't here, and he expects us to take care of ourselves until he returns. We have to be strong and make good decisions."

He nodded as he wiped the tears that spilled down his cheeks. "I... I heard Archer say he'd leave in the morning."

"Yes."

"But even if they go, I'm afraid they'll come back."

She wouldn't lie to him. "I believe they will also, so we must be prepared. When Matt was here, he took care to always keep an eye on the land, so it will be your responsibility to be the sentry from now on in his stead. Tomorrow, you find yourself a good observation place where you can see in every direction. That way, you'll be able to warn us in plenty of time if they return."

"But that's only good in the daytime. What about night?"

Brenna smiled. "Night is for you to rest and not worry. Papa, Grandpa, Uncle Pete, Jim, myself—all of us—will take turns for night watch."

"What if I can't warn you?"

Brenna thought a moment. "Then you hide in the barn just like you did today. Pick out several good hiding places. I'll figure out a way to get to you, but you wait there until I do. Don't try to come to any of the houses, no matter what."

Tears welled again, but he nodded.

Brenna kissed his forehead. "Now, go home the way you came in, and I'll lock the door behind you. I think Archer is good for his word about leaving in the morning." She squeezed his hand. It was going to be a long night.

Chapter Fifteen

During the three days of rest in Trinidad, Matt paid for a month of board and upkeep for John's old horse and purchased a good-natured gelding as a replacement. Samson needed a new set of shoes, and Matt dickered over the price of four outfitted pack mules, while John filled their supply list.

Matt's last stop before returning to the Colombian Hotel for a hot meal and a good night's rest was the mercantile and the ring he'd seen in the window display earlier in the day. The color had caught his notice—a golden band with two small inlaid sparkling sapphire gemstones as blue as Brenna's eyes.

With sunrise on the third morning, Matt led the way out of Trinidad and up the trail over Cuchara Pass. Although there were other shorter and more direct routes to his destination, this was the only way he'd come with Henry. If he had a chance of recognizing landmarks on the map or when he rode into the valley where they'd camped, it was going to be from this direction. Once he had the gold, he'd cut straight east out of the foothills to make up lost time, which would deliver them on the plains north of Hoehne. From there, he'd angle southeast cross-country to the ranch.

Legends of hidden treasure and lost caches of gold abounded in the West, and Matt had heard them all time and again from Henry. The story he knew best was of the old miner who came out of the hills every fall with a gold nugget big enough to live on for the coming year. It amused him that he now understood why it was Henry's favorite yarn.

Looking back now, he remembered when Henry had left him with friends in Tucson for a couple of months. When Henry returned, he'd taken Matt to Chicago for half-a-year. It must have been the last time the old man had gone for some gold. Matt shook his head as he recalled the good time they'd had in Chicago and the money they'd spent. That's where he'd had his first taste of whiskey, women, and gambling.

Matt glanced back at John following with the pack mules strung out behind him, and John gave a wave that he was doing all right. It was good having him along, despite his propensity to greet everyone he encountered and engage them in conversation when he found a willing talker. John liked people, and they took to him mostly because he didn't preach. Matt was pretty sure they appreciated that as much as he did.

The downside to traveling with a minister was their odd partnership garnered undue attention and outright questions. To lessen the rumors, Matt dropped comments here and there that he was John's guide on his pilgrimage into the mountains. A stretched truth, but John could live with it.

At sunset a day later, they came down on the north side of the west Spanish Peak. Pointing into the valley that spread out before them,

Matt explained, "Those are granite stone dikes—Dakota Wells and the Devil's Stairstep. I've seen a lot of years between the last time I was here and now, but I recall we need to camp in that sheltered cove across the way. We'll be in the general vicinity of where we need to start searching."

"I am looking forward to having my feet on the ground and a hot cup of coffee in my hands."

"You and me both, Parson. I've got some worries on my mind that you need to know about, and I can't put off telling you any longer."

***

It was full dark when Matt sat across the fire nursing his coffee and working around in his head what he needed to say. John finally prompted him.

"You're stewing. Perhaps if you simply talk, your thoughts will work themselves out."

"I am stewing." Matt gave him a half-grin. "After all these miles together and me listening to your stories and you listening to mine, you haven't asked why we're here. Aren't you curious?"

"Yes. I must admit I am, but I was confident you would tell me when you felt it appropriate, or if I needed to know. All you've said is we're looking for treasure, and since treasure is anything a person deems valuable, I didn't presume to guess what it is."

Matt handed the little wooden box to him. "Look through this, then ask your questions. You've followed along with me on faith. It's only fair you know the purpose, now."

When John finished reading the letter and perusing the map, he returned them to the box. "This is quite interesting. So, your intent when you locate the gold is to put it to good use, just as Henry requested."

Matt nodded. "There's a woman, Brenna Gérard, and a ranch east of Trinidad at the foot of Trinchera Pass, waiting for me. I need the gold to help keep the ranch going and to show Brenna and her family that I'm finished with my guns." He grinned. "Besides, when I left her, she told me I'd better come back with a preacher to marry us."

John smiled back. "I will be glad to oblige." He was quiet for a few moments. "Is there a town nearby?

"No. Trinidad is thirty some miles to the west and Hoehne is twenty-five or so." He explained the history of the compound and what brought the family from Philadelphia.

"Is seems reasonable the area may become even more populated."

"Some farmers settled up on Johnson Mesa. There are neighbors within half-a-day's ride or less. The compound is set up like a small town. It wouldn't take much to build it up so folks would come in and settle. In fact, the Stirlings are considering selling lots."

A slow smile brightened John's face. "This may well be my calling."

Matt saw where John's thinking was going. "It's wide-open for you."

John leaned forward, his eyes bright with the fervor of a man with hope in his heart and a mission in his mind. "Matt, I believe our paths crossed because my destiny is somehow influenced, perhaps linked, with yours. This is where I'm meant to stay."

"Well, you'd better slow down on your plans, because there's something else you need to know before you make any permanent decisions."

"Oh? You sound quite serious."

"I am. There's a man named Archer. We've got bad blood between us."

"As in gun-play bad blood?"

Matt nodded. "Yeah. And he wants the gold for himself. I saw him in Taos just before I bumped into you. My gut tells me he's not far away, waiting for me to come out of these hills."

"There is no sense looking for trouble where there may be none."

Matt threw out the dregs in his cup. "That's true, but it doesn't hurt to be on the look-out, just in case."

Staring off to the southeast, he imagined Brenna out on her porch looking up at the same night sky and wondering where he was and if he was coming home. "Time to turn in. We'll start searching at first light." In his thoughts, he said goodnight to Brenna, then went to his bedroll.

***

Two days later with no success, Matt had traversed the area so many times, he could do it blindfolded. He'd studied every foot of the vertical dike wall; he knew every crack and fissure in the ancient layers of rock and soil. With each passing hour, his patience thinned and a little more hope died.

Now, as he sat at the campfire with coffee cup in hand with night coming on, he listened to the droning hum of the wind through the trees and grass, while studying the timberline ridge trail on the west peak, and admiring the scattered groves of Aspens that were well into their vibrant, seasonal color change.

With the map at his feet, Matt checked time and again to reassure himself he was in the right location. The granite dikes and the west peak rising up beyond were easy to spot on the map, but he couldn't make sense of the groups of circles spaced out in clumps, and the landmarks Henry had drawn just weren't out here anymore.

Matt talked aloud to work through his frustration. "I've been trying to put my mind back to what this land looked like all those years ago. I was a kid, and I didn't pay as much attention as Henry kept telling me to. It doesn't look all that different, yet it's changed. If that makes sense."

"It does. I understand what you mean."

Matt tapped his forefinger on the map. "We haven't found this—the hole or cave here in the dike with the two big rocks on each side and one tall tree concealing the hole."

"Or it could be a crevice," John offered.

Matt nodded. "Or crevice. And I can't make sense of these clusters of little circles."

John moved closer to study the map with Matt. "Let's think about Henry's circumstances at the time he hid the gold. He was pursued, which meant he didn't have time to spare, so he hid the gold in a hurry, and he had to choose landmark clues that would withstand years of weathering."

"That's the problem. Landmarks and the lay of the land change over the years. Trees grow or get struck by lightning, forests burn, rock slides alter the path of trails." Matt looked at John. "And cached gold is found by someone else." He needed that gold to be there. Not just for Henry or even himself now, because it didn't matter. He was taking off his guns for her with or without the gold. It was Brenna and her family he was thinking of.

John encouraged him. "Don't dwell on the what-ifs. Think of possibilities and solutions, instead."

Matt knew he was right, and he appreciated John's reminder. "Henry was worn out and so were the mules and his horse. His nerves were shot. He was feeling guilty about killing his partner. So he found a hole, stashed the gold, made a rough sketch of the location, and took off before anyone saw him." He refilled his coffee cup as he thought it over. "But any way we look at it, there isn't a tall tree in front of a cave with two big rocks on either side. You've looked as much as I have."

Matt closed his eyes, and brought up memories of walking the trail along the dike, fishing in the shallow stream that wound through the valley, and reading to Henry by firelight. Shaking his head, he looked at John. "Nothing. I'm coming up—"

John leaned forward with the anticipation of a kid waiting for the end of a suspenseful story, his spectacles reflecting the firelight. "You've thought of something."

"Not a clue, more of advice Henry told me. He said people overlook what's in plain sight because in their heads, they've already decided what they ought to see, even when it's wrong, and they know it."

"So we're blinded by the limits we concocted in our minds."

"Something like that. Tomorrow, we won't look for hidden treasure or holes or rocks. We'll just...look."

Rolling up in his blankets, the urgency of time running out gnawed at him. The milky veil over the stars promised snowfall, and that would bring an end to searching until springtime. If he didn't find the gold tomorrow, he wouldn't find it at all. He'd known men who had wasted their lives lured by the temptation to look just one more time and that once more became another and another... Eventually, they died with nothing to show but the glitter of greed for all their troubles. He wasn't cursed with gold fever, but going back to Brenna empty-handed was a prospect that stung his pride.

***

Matt awoke in the dark minutes just before dawn to still cold air, a dusting of snow, and the feel of a storm bearing down. He got a fire and coffee going without waking John, then hunkered into his coat while he squatted at the edge of the fire with jerked beef and hardtack. When the coffee was ready, he poured a cup and inhaled the pungent aroma rising on the steam—and froze. Off to the side, just out of his direct vision, Matt sensed a shadow where none had been. Then, the air rippled on an instant of breeze, and a man appeared at the edge of the firelight circle. A few weeks ago,

seeing Gregory had scared the hell out of him. Now, he thought of
him as an old friend.

"John. Wake up." Matt tugged at the foot of John's blankets to
rouse him. "We've got company."

John fumbled for his spectacles. "What? A visitor? Where?"

Matt jerked a nod. "To your left at the edge of camp."

John peered, adjusted his spectacles, and whispered out of the
corner of his mouth. "Why is he just standing there?"

"That's what I'm trying to figure out."

Squinting and bobbing his head, John said, "He seems familiar,
now that I look at him more closely."

"He's the man we were both following when I bumped into you."

"Yes. I see that now. This is most unusual. Why did he follow us?
And why doesn't he speak? It's unnerving how he's watching us."
John dragged his attention from the stranger to look at Matt.

"His name's Gregory Gérard. Brenna's dead husband." Matt cut
a sidelong glance at John. The parson's face went white as the snow
on his blankets.

"You...you mean he's a gh—ghost?"

"Yep."

John swallowed hard, his gaze riveted on Gregory. "Is he of a
malevolent nature or amiable?"

"I've pondered that one myself. A few months ago, I was riding
the fence on that very question, but after encountering him in Taos,
I made up my mind he's more of a guardian angel than a ghost. He
kept me from likely getting myself killed a few minutes before he put
you in my path. He watches over Brenna. I think he's helping me get

back to her with my hide intact, and you along with me. I'd venture a guess he's trying to tell us something right now."

With that, Gregory put his back to the camp and walked away with the first glow of sunrise lightening the horizon.

"Like I said." Matt stood and gave John a hand up. "Get the pack mules ready, grab coffee and a bite to eat. After the sun's up, bring the mules along. I have a feeling we're about to find some gold."

Matt grabbed his rifle and followed Gregory down the same game trail he and John had walked countless times. Gregory covered the ground in a steady pace, and Matt kept a keen eye on him, hardly blinking for fear of losing sight of him.

When Gregory stopped, Matt broke into a trot with a jagged chunk of granite jutting up as his reference to Gregory's location. In the time it took Matt to climb his way around and over a rock slide that had cracked off from the dike years ago, Gregory was gone.

Matt scanned the ground where Gregory had stopped. Nothing. Just a handful of egg-sized, smooth round stones— On the map...circles in a cluster, small rocks in a pile. His heart took a few rapid beats, and he knelt to dig dirt and grass from around the pile of stones to find four individual stones placed end-to-end on one side like an arrow pointing the way. Matt pulled out the map and compared the circles at the bottom of the map to the rocks. Now, it made sense.

He walked on, studying the trail. He found the next pile of stones with the three leader rocks pointing farther along the way he was going. He estimated where he'd find the pile of stones with two rocks indicating the way, but even doubling back and rechecking every inch of the trail from the previous marker, he couldn't find it.

Undaunted, he moved on. The last pile of stones was plain as could be and larger than the others. So large, he stood on it yesterday without a suspicion of what it was. The arrow-rock at this pile pointed toward the dike instead of the trail.

Matt was embarrassed to think how many times he'd walked right over, and stepped on, Henry's clues the past two days and never saw them for what they were.

Gazing up the steep slope, a smile broke over his face. "Well, I'll be damned."

A boulder perched big as life beside the stump of a lightning-charred pine. On the other side of the burned tree, what was left of a boulder looked down upon a sizeable piece that had split and rolled ten feet farther on. Matt took a few steps to the side. A crevice his height with an opening that appeared wide enough for a man to squeeze through, stood out plain and inviting.

Matt waited in that spot until John brought the mules up. "We passed this place fifty times, and we couldn't see what was right in front of us." Grinning, he slapped John on the shoulder. "Let's go up and bring out Henry's gold."

Chapter Sixteen

Sunset and solitude settled over the Stirling Compound. With the season's first freeze two weeks past, the days since had turned Indian Summer warm, but this evening, the air held the feel and promise of a change in the weather. Walking along the stone path, Brenna smiled at the jack-o'-lanterns Drew had placed upon door steps, porch railings, and the summer table. She'd helped him carve the pumpkins two days ago. It was odd he hadn't lit the candles yet.

He was excited for Halloween, and she had a party planned for him. Halloween festivities were popular back east, and she wanted to continue the tradition at the ranch. His friend, Dara's youngest brother, Billy Everett, was coming over in the morning to spend a few days.

Glancing about, she saw her father crossing the yard from the bath house, and Jim returning from checking the perimeter walls and all the compound gates they'd kept closed day and night since Archer's visit. But where was Drew? It was suppertime, and unlike him to be late for a meal, let alone far from the house this close to dark.

Brenna strolled on toward the barn for a last search of the hen that hadn't gone in to roost a half-hour ago. Even if that crotchety old biddy was still out, she'd close up anyway. Better to lose one chicken to coyotes than the whole flock.

As always when she walked about, her gaze moved over the mesas and on to the snowcapped mountains to the west. Was Matt up there in that high, rough country searching for gold? Had he found it—and was he on his way home?

Tonight, she especially missed him. Just this morning she'd felt the quickening—the first time she'd carried a baby long enough to feel its first movements—and she ached to share it with him. This baby would thrive. She sent out her thoughts along with a heart full of wishes for his soon, and safe, return.

An explosion of light and with a deafening sound threw Brenna flat on her back as if an invisible hand had slapped her. Chunks of rocks, wood, and dirt pelted around her. Dust rose and swirled in a dirty, choking cloud. Gasping for air, Brenna rolled to her knees. Her father's voice, distant and hollow, called her name. Then, he was at her side, helping her stand. Her ears rang; the world twisted and tilted in her vision. James held her steady until she could stand on her own.

"Are you hurt?"

Brenna wavered, shook her head. "No...no. I'm all right. What was that?"

"Dynamite."

"Get to the storm cellar. I'm going for a shotgun." Jim went by on a dead run with four dogs passing him in their frantic race for the safety of Brenna's porch.

Two men on foot materialized out of the dust and came at them with guns drawn. One fired over their heads. Another yelled, "Stay where you are. Put your hands up."

Jim made a mad leap for Brenna's porch, but a bullet smashed into a porch post in front of him, peppering him with splinters. He ducked and stopped, his hands raised.

"Another trick like that, cowboy, and it'll be the last thing you ever do. Mosey on back and stand with these two while we wait."

"Wait for what?" James demanded. "We welcome travelers. There was no need to blow up the gates."

"We had our doubts we'd be welcome. There's someone coming in who likes the way dynamite gets folks' attention. Leaves 'em with no doubt about his intentions."

Brenna sucked in a gasp. Archer. Of course. She recognized these two men, now. The one doing the talking was the older man she'd heard Archer call Walt.

James demanded, "What is your purpose here?"

"You'll know soon enough. Keep your hands where I can see them, and we'll get along just fine."

Brenna dabbed at the bloody specks on Jim's face with the hem of her apron and picked out splinters from his cheek and neck.

Jim whispered, "Where's Drew?"

Brenna shrugged. Her fear was Archer had captured him. Then, she remembered the plan they'd made for just such a situation.

Shaking as much from relief as from the explosion, she whispered, "Hiding in the barn. Somehow I have to get to him—alone."

Brenna heard the galloping hoof beats long before Archer rode into the compound ahead of another man who had two saddled horses in tow. Archer stopped in front of her and touched the front of his hat in greeting.

"'Evening, Mrs. Gérard. Nice night for a social call, wouldn't you say?"

"Do you expect me to answer honestly, Mr. Archer?"

Archer chuckled. "So you do know who I am."

With her natural boldness and a desire to regain a modicum of control, she said, "Yes. I knew who you were the first time you were here. Matt warned me to watch for a man who wears his guns for a border draw and rides a flashy sorrel paint horse."

"What else did he say about me?"

"You used to be saddle partners."

Archer nodded. "Then you know why I'm here."

"I know you and he did not part friends."

"Well, I won't deny it." Moving his gaze to James, he asked, "Who else is here?"

"No one."

Archer cocked his head, eyeing him. "I don't like liars. Can't trust them. I happen to know there are other womenfolk here and an old couple—maybe more—and you've got ranch hands."

Jim stepped up. "He's not lying. It's just us. The rest of our family went to Colorado Springs early in the week to meet my sister coming in from Philadelphia. They won't be home for days."

Archer considered that. "The hired hands?"

"Some are out on the range. Most are helping neighbors raise a barn. They'll stay for the party they're throwing to celebrate tomorrow night. We'll have a full crew back in a couple of days."

"Where's the boy?"

Brenna spoke up before Jim or her father had a chance. "He left this morning for his friend's house. It's about ten miles from here."

"We'll be staying in your house, Mrs. Gérard. I like your cooking. Get supper ready while Herker puts up our horses and makes a check through all the buildings just in case someone's hiding." He eyed Brenna. "This is your only chance to call-in anyone else so they don't get hurt if they get a notion to play hero."

Brenna just looked at him, her gaze steady in her refusal to yield to his threat.

Satisfied, Archer said, "The rest of us will go inside and get to know each other better while you cook. I want hot coffee. Lots of it, and keep it coming. You three play nice, and we'll be on our way before you know it, just like we promised last time, and no one will be the worse for wear."

Dismounting, he handed the reins to Herker. "When you're done in the barn, come to the house and take first watch on the porch. Walt, Vernon, check the men for guns, then escort these fine folks to the house."

Brenna reached the kitchen door first, and Archer cautioned, "I suspect you've got that sawed-off shotgun by the door where you can lay hands on it. Best you leave it alone."

Brenna didn't acknowledge him and went straight to the stove to put on a second pot of coffee.

Once inside, Archer assessed the area with a sweeping study from the closed root cellar door beneath his feet and the guns on the wall to the piano on back to the fireplace.

"Vernon, Walt, drag those two chairs by the fireplace over closer, and find something to tie these two gents in them." He nudged Jim forward. "I don't want to hear a sound out of you two. It might tempt me to use you as target practice." He looked at the guns again. "Then get those weapons off the wall and stow them down in the root cellar. While you're down there, look around for other guns."

To Brenna, he asked, "You heard from Caddock since we were here?"

"No."

"Speak up and look at me when you talk."

Brenna took her time mending the stove fire before facing him. "Nothing has changed since you were here last. He rode out one morning, and I don't know when, or if, he'll return." She made herself meet the hard gaze he leveled upon her despite her urge to look away.

Finally, he nodded. "I believe you." He took a seat at the kitchen table, leaned the chair back on two legs, and propped his feet on the tabletop. "I've got a story I think you'll find interesting. After I left here, I rode down to Folsom, then over to Raton and up to Trinidad asking around about Caddock. I found out he left Trinidad with a weeks' worth of supplies and four pack mules. That tells me he expects to come out of the mountains before the first hard snow."

He paused and placed one of his revolvers on the table then took the other one out and rolled the cylinder.

"There's only one reason he'd go into the mountains this time of year. He's looking for a cache of gold, and he'll bring it straight here."

"You're certainly confident you know what he'll do."

Archer nodded. "I rode with Matt long enough to know what he'll fight for and what he won't. One thing I know for sure is that a man like Caddock doesn't leave a woman like you behind. Not for any amount of gold." He studied the revolver up close then glanced at Brenna again.

"Curious thing. Along with the mules and supplies, there was another man with him—a preacher-man. Now, since I also know Caddock bought a woman's ring before he headed into the high country, I'm banking on him being a man so in love that there's no stopping him from coming back here. He'll trade the gold for you, ain't no doubt about that, or I'll kill him and take it. Makes no never mind to me"

Turning to conceal her relief, Brenna closed her eyes on a deep breath and allowed herself a little smile. Matt was coming back. But her moment of happiness dissolved, for she knew in her heart Archer didn't intend to let Matt live. Composed, she commented, "You may have to wait quite a while before he returns. Are you prepared to keep us, and our hired hands when they return, hostage indefinitely?"

"That's where you're wrong." Archer spun the cylinder on the revolver again then pointed it at the kitchen door with one eye squinted as he peered down the length of the barrel. "It snowed hard on the Peaks a day or two ago. I'm betting Caddock's coming out of the mountains right now, and he's headed here. It'll be a day, maybe two, and this will be all over."

Brenna placed a stack of plates with tableware in front of Archer along with a coffee pot and cups. She served them food the same way—in bowls from which they could serve themselves. She wasn't about to play waitress for them. She did, however, fill a plate and coffee cup for Walt who thanked her when she took it to him. Then, she went about fixing two more plates, which she arranged on a serving platter around two cups of coffee. She hadn't taken three steps when Archer stopped her.

"Where are you going with those?"

"No one goes hungry in my house. I'm sure my father and brother want supper. I understand we are your hostages, but that does not preclude my attention to them or their needs." She met Archer's hard gaze straight on. "It will be necessary to loosen their bonds so they may eat."

Archer took his time considering. "All right. Keep it straight with me, lady, and I'll keep it straight with you."

"Thank you for your consideration."

"Herker, untie one of their arms."

When Herker went back to the table, Brenna helped Jim and James situate the plates across their knees, and she placed the coffee cups on the floor within reach.

Jim whispered, "You're doing fine, Sis, just fine."

James nodded encouragement.

"Hey, woman!" Vernon lifted the coffee pot. "Bring over the fresh coffee. This pot's empty."

Stiff-backed, Brenna placed the serving platter on the counter, picked up the fresh pot of coffee from the stove, and went to the table. Vernon, leering with yellow, tobacco-stained teeth, held his cup so she had to lean into him to fill it. She swallowed hard to keep from gagging at the stench rising from his body. As she stepped back, he grabbed her and pulled her to his lap as he wrapped a meaty arm around her waist.

"Not so fast."

He nuzzled her neck, sending her into a reeling exodus. Seizing a fork from his plate, she impaled it into the fleshy curve between his thumb and forefinger, pinning his hand to the wooden table as she tore loose from his grip in the same motion that she dumped the coffee in his lap. The big man howled and jumped up, knocking his chair over in his frantic grab at the fork while dancing around from the scalding.

Backing from the table, her gaze locked on Vernon, Brenna reached for the knuckleduster tucked inside her pocket...then good sense intervened. This wasn't the time.

Whirling, she snatched the carving knife from the cutting board and held it low at her side, ready to bring the tip up and into Vernon's soft belly.

Vernon yanked the fork out and came around the table screaming and cursing. With the sink and counter at her back, she steeled herself for Vernon's attack and the one chance she'd have to stop him. Then Archer was between them, his guns drawn with such speed she hadn't seen him do it.

"Leave her alone."

The look in Vernon's eyes was a shade off of crazy, and Brenna thought he'd bull right over Archer to get to her. She wished he would. If Archer didn't kill him, she would.

A spark of sanity made its way into Vernon's head, and he backed down, but not without complaint. "Damn it! Look what she did." Blood dripped from his hand.

"Quit your bellyaching. You had it coming."

Brenna warned, "If he attempts to touch me again, I will spill his guts onto his feet."

Archer looked at her, a slow smile spreading over his face when he saw the knife in her hand. "And I think you'd be successful." Holstering one gun, he held out his empty hand.

Brenna hesitated. Not because she intended to keep the knife. That was a ludicrous idea, given the circumstances. But because her whole body trembled, and she didn't want Archer or Vernon to see her hands shake. Archer waited, his expression revealing nothing, but his eyes darkening just enough she knew she was pushing his patience.

Relinquishing the knife, she busied herself at making another pot of coffee, her stomach churning and her legs unsteady.

"Damn it, Archer—"

"Shut up and sit down. Or go outside and wash off the blood. Caddock thinks highly of womenfolk. Why the hell do you think I bothered coming here instead of laying for him along the trail? It'd be a gunfight with nothing gained. But not here. She's our ace in this game.

"As long as Caddock's convinced she hasn't been messed with, I guarantee he'll do whatever I want to keep her that way. But if he suspects she's been harmed, all bets are off with him. He'll go crazy-mad. I've seen him walk into gunfire reloading his empty guns as calmly as if it was a cake walk at a Sunday church social. He doesn't scare on a normal day, and he damn well doesn't scare when he's mad. I intend to live until I'm an old man spending his gold. I suggest you do the same."

Archer tapped the barrel of his revolver on Vernon's chest. "Touch her again before I'm finished with Caddock and I'll hold you while she cuts off some body parts you're proud of. She's not for your enjoyment unless, or until, I say so." He cast a warning glance at Brenna then back to Vernon. "Both of you remember that."

She understood and, for now, appreciated the tenuous protection he offered. Putting her mind to the mundane task of cleaning up supper dishes allowed her to work through a way to get to the barn to talk to Drew. She couldn't let him stay out there all night worrying, and she needed to get him away from the compound and to safety.

Wiping her hands on her apron, she carried the two buckets of dishwater that had drained from the sink and set them at the door.

Facing Archer, she said, "I need to throw-out this dirty water, and I was on my way to the barn to finish chores when you...arrived." She started to say blew up the gates, but caught herself. Purposely baiting him would get her nowhere. Holding her breath that he wouldn't come with her or send one of his men along, she waited.

Archer looked a long time at Jim and James before he answered. "All right. I think you're good for your word." Swinging his gaze to her, he added, "Use your imagination on what you'll find in here if you take too long."

Brenna forced a polite thank you. Grabbing the bucket bails, she backed through the screen door and carried them to the kitchen garden, tossed them out, and set them aside to pick up on her return. Taking a lantern from a peg on a porch post, she struck a match from the tin holder, lit the wick, and headed across the yard to the barn with her dogs scampering along with her.

The lantern light cast an eerie shadow over the gaping hole in the wall, and she shuddered that it was through Archer's twisted whim of fancy that she and Jim and her father were still alive. He could just as easily wait for Matt and the gold with the three of them dead.

When she reached the barn, she cut a quick glance behind to make sure she wasn't followed.

"Drew!" she called in a loud whisper. Nothing. She called again, louder. Still nothing. Filling a grain bucket, she climbed through the corral rails and dumped grain into the tubs to use the gathered horses as cover as she peered into the darkness for Drew.

"Brenna!"

She nearly dropped the bucket. "Where are you?"

"By the windmill."

Brenna hurried to him, wrapping him into an embrace of relief and tears. Clutching her, his words came fast and breathy.

"I saw something moving out there, but the sun was in my eyes and I couldn't tell what it was. Then a few minutes later, the gates exploded. I started to run out to you, but then I saw two men leading horses riding hard toward us. I—I didn't have time to warn you. I just hid here like you told me to."

His body trembled, and she hugged him more tightly. "Oh, Drew. You made the right decision. I'm so glad you're safe."

"I sneaked around to the back of your house and listened at one of the portals. The cover wasn't latched so I pushed it open just enough that I could see some of what was going on. I heard everything. When Archer said you could come out to do chores, I ran back here."

"Come into the barn."

Standing in a shadowed corner, Brenna grasped Drew's hands. "I need you to ride to the Everetts' and tell them what's happening here. Mr. Everett will know what to do." That wasn't a complete lie, but she knew it was the only way to convince Drew to leave. By the time anyone could alert the sheriff in Trinidad and get a posse out here, Archer would be long gone—or it wouldn't matter. In that event, the undertaker would be the only person to notify.

Bright tears of fear shone in his eyes. "But...but I've never been out at night all alone. I don't know what to do."

Brenna took hold of his shoulders with a tighter grip than she meant, but her own terror drove her to get Drew out of danger. "Remember what Matt told you when at first you were afraid to go on the cattle drive?"

Drew nodded. "He said a person doesn't know what he can or can't do until he has to do it."

"That's right. When Matt was exactly your age, his father was killed right beside him from a Comanche arrow. Matt didn't know what to do. Just like you, now. So he did the only thing he could do—what he *had* to do. He kept on fighting for his father. He picked up his father's rifle and started shooting back. That's what you have to do now. You have to fight for us."

Drew wiped his face on his shirt sleeve, nodding.

"Hide until it's well past bedtime, then ride Speckles to Billy's house. She's tame as a kitten. Walk her away from here for at least half-a-mile so no one hears you. Then, go as fast as you can. Don't stop for anything."

"I've never ridden Speckles. Can't I take Socks?"

"No. Archer will notice he's gone."

The kitchen door slammed. Brenna cut a glance that way, then kissed Drew's forehead. One more hug and she urged, "Hide."

When she picked up the lantern, the light fell on the spare shotgun just an arm's length away. Her heart and her mind waged war. With her hand an inch from the weapon, a fleeting breath floating on a whisper warned, *Remember the baby you carry*. She sucked in a sharp breath. So many days had passed without sensing Gregory's presence she thought he'd gone for good.

On an equally soft whisper, she said, "You're right. Thank you." It was the reminder she needed that to challenge Archer and lose would be certain death for Jim and her father, and unspeakable brutality for her before they killed her. Pressing her palm against the knuckleduster, she found strength in the knowledge that she had seven bullets with Vernon's name on them.

Crossing in front of the barn doors on the way to the chicken house, Brenna cut a sidelong glance to see Archer a few yards away, but she didn't break stride or acknowledge his approach. Holding the lantern to illuminate the inside of the chicken house, she made a head-count. The old hen had come in to roost. Good. She dropped the small slider door into place and locked them in.

"Took your time." Archer watched from doorway.

On an exaggerated, impatient sigh, she said, "Mr. Archer. When one is searching for a stubborn hen that doesn't want to roost with the others, it takes a bit of time. Morning chores will take much longer. I suggest if you don't care for the way I do chores, then you should do the milking yourself." Her impatience, steeped as it was in worry for Drew, pushed her temper past good sense to keep a civil tongue. "And while we're speaking of milking, in order to prepare meals, I will need to go into the root cellar. Perhaps storing my guns down there wasn't your best planning."

He laughed outright. "You are a bold woman, Mrs. Gérard. I like that. You just tell me what you need, and I'll personally fetch it for you."

She shut half of the double barn doors, which prompted him to step out of the way as she closed the other half.

He grabbed the door. "I saw something moving in there."

Brenna chided, "Of course, you did. It's a barn. We have cats and dogs."

"No. It was bigger. Looked like a man-sized shadow."

For a moment, she was taken aback. Surely Gregory hadn't shown himself to Archer. Fearing Archer would take the lantern and search the barn, Brenna didn't wait for him. Calling the dogs, she assumed a lackadaisical manner and headed for the house, swinging the lantern as if she hadn't a care in the world on such a fine autumn night.

"Please drop the bar into place when you're finished prowling about, and draw the gates closed."

Resisting the urge to look back, it wasn't until she heard his footsteps that she breathed easier. No longer worried that he'd find Drew, she set about figuring a way to convince Archer to untie her brother and father. If they were going to die at Archer's hands, it wouldn't be as sitting ducks. They deserved a fighting chance to live. And fight, they would, if given the opportunity.

Chapter Seventeen

At daylight the second morning out of the mountains, Matt poured a cup of re-warmed coffee, then dug out the last of the jerked meat, hard tack, and what was left of the bacon from last night's supper.

From the feel in the air and the overcast sunrise, he was mere hours ahead of the snow. He'd planned to push on through the night, but exhaustion overrode urgency, and he'd made camp. Bone-weary, he could only imagine how tired John was, and they'd run out of grain for the horses and mules a day ago.

Matt scratched his bearded chin, knowing he needed a shave and a haircut, not to mention a change of clothes. The lure of dropping south and doubling-back to Hoehne for a meal and hot bath tempted him. With this early of a start, he could afford the time. He hated showing up at the ranch looking as rough as the day Brenna had dragged him out of the creek, and he suspected several days without a bath wasn't going to get him an invitation to her bed. He chuckled. Hell, nothing was keeping him from her bed tonight.

John stirred and rolled out of his blankets.

"G'mornin', Parson."

"Good morning, Matt."

Matt handed John a cup of coffee and nodded toward the jerky, hardtack, and bacon. "This is the last of it. Are you up for riding straight on in? If you're not, there's a town not far out of our way."

John scooted closer to the fire and rubbed his hands together over the flames. "How many miles is it to the ranch?"

"Twenty, give or take."

"Oh, that's not far at all. I know how eager you are to go on. I'll manage just fine. I've become quite adept at sleeping in the saddle."

Matt smiled. John had been a tenderfoot when he'd bumped into him in Taos, but he'd shaped up to be a man to ride with.

"The land's not too rough from here on in. We'll make good time once we cross the Picketwire."

"Picketwire? Is that a boundary around someone's land?"

Matt grinned. "No. It's a river."

"That's an odd name for a river."

"There's a legend about how the river came to be called the Picketwire. A couple hundred years ago or more, some Spanish militia, along with a group of priests, rode up out of Mexico looking for the source of stories they'd heard about gold around the Spanish Peaks—which, back then, were known by other names. Mexican Mountains, Twin Peaks, *Dos Hermanos*... I've heard the Ute, Comanche, and Apache thought they were a spiritual place, and they called them *Wahatoya*, which means Breasts of the Earth.

"Anyway, it took these Spaniards a while, but they made it to the Peaks and found a rich vein somewhere in the high country west of Trinidad. They forced some local Indians to do the digging, then killed them and high-tailed it out with the gold.

"Well, those soldiers and priests came over Cuchara Pass and followed the Purgatoire River, but they were in too much of a hurry to get out of the mountains, and they got lost. Somewhere out here on the plains where the Purgatoire cuts through some rough breaks, Indians ambushed that greedy bunch and killed the lot of them. Men have searched for that lost gold up and down the river, but no one's ever found it. It was a helluva treacherous river, so it came to be called *Rio de las Animas Perdido en Purgatorio*—"

"Oh! River of Souls Lost in Purgatory."

Matt arched an eyebrow. "You speak Mexican?"

"Acceptably well, yes."

Matt nodded. "That's good to know. Well, later when the French trappers came along, they changed the river's name to *Purgatoire*. Pardon my lousy French. Then, the English-speaking settlers who passed through or settled here thought that fancy French word sounded more like Picketwire. And that's what stuck."

John smiled. "What a delightful anecdote. I have so much to learn about the West and its ways. I'm looking forward to learning."

"Well, you've had a good education since Taos."

"That, I have—and I'm grateful to you for it."

"Eat up and finish off the coffee, then we'll pack up and hit the trail."

***

Midday found them with the Picketwire at their backs, and Matt's sights set on the northern rim of McBride Butte, which was close enough to make out the outlines of individual trees. In just a few more miles, he'd be home. It was the first time since his mother had died that he'd considered any place home, and the only time he'd ever had someone waiting for him. It was a good feeling that warmed him way down inside.

Scanning the land in his constant vigil, he spied movement some miles ahead. Field glasses to his face, he honed in on the area. A horse with rider and a buckboard with two people. Jerking the glasses down, he called over his shoulder to John.

"People coming this way and moving right along. I'm going on to meet them. Don't hurry the mules with their loads. Come at your own speed. I'll wait for you."

Matt took off at a gallop. He recognized the horse and rider an instant before Drew stood in his stirrups, yelling and waving madly. Matt reined in and Drew jumped off his filly and ran toward him. Matt hit the ground and gathered the boy into his arms.

"Drew! What's wrong?"

"Matt! It's awful. They need your help!"

Asa Everett brought the buckboard to a stop. "Matt, there's trouble at the compound. We're headed to Trinidad for the sheriff. Don't know what good it'll do, but I don't see there's any other way. We'll get a posse rounded up and head back out."

"Posse? What happened?"

Stuttering, but gaining confidence as he told the story, Drew recounted every detail from the night Archer first stopped in to his return and plan to kill Matt for the gold and the threat to let Vernon have Brenna.

Matt looked toward the ranch where it lay over the rolling hills and out of sight. A cold, empty anger started to build inside his chest. Archer had pushed his greed too far, and there was only one way to end it.

"You're going to kill Archer, aren't you?"

Matt lowered his gaze to see hope and fear all mixed up in Drew's face. Nodding, Matt said, "Yes. I am."

"I'm going back with you."

"No, Drew. You have to stay with Billy and his pa. When you get to Trinidad, stay there. I'll come get you when it's over." Matt put a hand on Drew's shoulder. "You took on a man's heart when you went for help. I couldn't have done better." He didn't want Drew to see what Matt feared awaited at the ranch. There were some sights a kid shouldn't have burned into his memories.

Matt slipped his Winchester from the scabbard and dug in his saddle bags for a box of shells and dumped out a handful. "A man needs his own weapon." He handed the rifle to Drew and put the shells into the boy's coat pocket. "It's loaded. Use it like I taught you."

Drew took a solid hold on the Winchester with both hands. "You say that like I won't see you again." His voice caught in his throat.

Matt mounted then looked down at Drew. "It'll take a better man than Archer to stop me." With a nod of thanks to Asa, he rode out to intercept John.

"I'm headed up on the plateau. It'll be tough going from here on in." He explained what happened. "This is my fight. I don't expect you to go the rest of the way."

John tapped the Bible he held tucked under his arm. "I think you need both of us now more than you ever have in your life. Lead the way. I will be right behind you."

Matt nodded. "I think you may be right, Parson. I think you may be right."

***

Matt sat in the cover of a stand of pines and watched the compound through his field glasses, running through his options and coming up short. The few things he knew for certain were grim. Vernon had a reputation for ruining women; then, often as not, killing them or leaving them in such a state they wished they were dead. From Drew's description of Brenna defending herself against Vernon's assault, he'd make sure Archer wasn't around to stop him when he made his move on her again. That made Vernon number one for who Matt was going to kill first.

Walt and Herker would stand in a fight, but they'd also take care to lay low if it meant saving their own skins. As for Archer, Matt had never seen anyone faster on the draw, but fast was Archer's weakness. He valued speed over accuracy, and accuracy was Matt's advantage.

With the rest of the family out of danger—which Matt counted as a boon despite Brenna, Jim, and James being hostages—he'd not expected to see much activity in the yard, and he was right. What he observed went a long way in easing his worry, and it also brought up questions.

Over the space of two hours, Brenna had thrown dishwater out on the garden plot, called the dogs inside, and brought food, maybe coffee, to Jim and James where they idled at the porch step, sometimes standing, other times sitting, but always under guard.

Matt pegged the location of Archer's men—one at the rubble where the gate had been, watching the land; another walking sentry duty; and the third, guarding Jim and James. He thought he detected movement in the shadows of the porch, which was probably Archer. His main question was why was everyone but Brenna outside?

As afternoon wore on to dusk, a light mist moved in, and with it came a sharp drop in temperature. It wouldn't be long before mist turned to freezing drizzle. Matt was sure it would snow by dark, and that was the one thing he couldn't shake off. Dark was too late. He'd promised to return before the first snowfall.

Removing a little velvet-covered ring box from his coat pocket, Matt flipped the lid open on its hinge. He ran his thumb over the gemstones, and it was all he needed to make up his mind what to do. He'd always believed the only way to handle a fight was to walk right up and face it. There was no sense waiting. It was time he took the fight to Archer, and let the bodies fall where they may.

Matt returned the box to his pocket. He looked at John where he sat hunkered down in his heavy wool coat with collar turned up around his ears, and his hat pulled low over his brow. Somewhere along the miles, he'd come to think of John as a friend. He'd known men he liked and respected, but other than Henry and the men in Brenna's family, there'd been few enough he'd called true friends, and even fewer he'd trust with his life. John was one of the very few, and he'd be a lucky man if John thought the same of him.

"Gather up, Parson. We're going in."

"Now?" John pushed up his spectacles. "You said we should wait until after dark to surprise them. You said it was too dangerous in daylight. Even...certain death."

With a wry smile, Matt said, "Then it's a damn good thing you're with me. You can say some nice words over my grave."

"Matt, this is nothing to joke about."

"You're right, but it's true, nonetheless."

Matt tightened his saddle cinch, put the field glasses in the saddle bag, and brought out a piece of torn, tied-up burlap roughly the size of a man's fist and filled with gold nuggets. Tossing it to John, he said, "In case I don't make it. Something for your troubles."

John didn't open the sack. "It has not been troublesome. Friendship has kept me with you in your quest."

Matt walked to him with the other item he'd taken from the saddlebag. John looked at him, then at the revolver.

Shaking his head, he said, "I've never held a gun. I wouldn't know how to use it. And I don't believe I could take a life."

"Even if it meant saving your own?"

John tapped his Bible. "All the protection I need is in here."

"Unless you can wear that book like a piece of armor and it can stop bullets, the six shots in this gun may be a better choice to get you through this alive." Matt took John's hand and slapped the gun on his palm. "Tuck it into your trousers where you can reach it. When this plays out, it may be up to you to help the rest of the Stirling family go on..." Matt swallowed the tight lump in his throat and blew out a hard breath.

John placed a hand on Matt's arm. "You can count on me to help where I'm needed."

"John, if I don't make it back to her, finish this for me." Matt held out the velvet box. "Tell her I didn't leave her alone. Tell her I didn't take the gold and run."

He looked at the box then at Matt. "May I?"

Matt nodded.

John opened the box. For a few seconds, he smiled and nodded, then tucked the box into his coat pocket. "I will, Matt. I'll make sure she knows."

Once packed, mounted, and ready to move out, Matt said, "I've been thinking. Brenna's sister is around your age. She's got college-trained medical skills and is eager to put them to good use. Maybe the two of you can hook-up and help civilize this land together."

John's face blazed red. "I—I'm not looking for a—"

"Wife?" Matt grinned. "I wasn't either, but if Corrine is half the woman her sister is, propose to her when you meet her so she doesn't get away."

"The love of a good woman?"

Matt nodded. "That's right." Turning Samson toward home, he said, "Let's ride."

Winding their way to the bottom of the butte, Matt picked up an occasional word on the wintry breeze that he recognized as John reciting a prayer Matt had heard a few times. It involved walking through a valley and shadow of death. If he lived long enough, he'd ask John to explain just what that prayer meant. When they reached the flat, John was part-singing, part-humming what sounded like a hymn. Something about soldiers marching on to war. Matt wasn't hopeful the end of the battle would find his soul on its way to heaven no matter how much the Parson prayed and sang.

Some souls couldn't be saved, and he was pretty sure he'd lost his chance years ago.

Chapter Eighteen

Matt was mad. Mad at himself for bringing this trouble to Brenna, and mad at Archer for his bloodthirsty greed. He knew only one way to end this, and death hung low on his thighs. Matt could take a slug and keep going. He'd done it before. When he pulled the trigger, his shots counted. Every time. Archer and his men were not leaving the Stirling ranch alive, even if he had to die to make it happen.

Matt rode with his toes at the edge of his stirrups, ready to leave the saddle in a hurry. Aware of the rifles following him the last mile to the compound, he kept his hands in plain sight and advised John to do the same. With a sweeping gaze, Matt pinned the location of each person. Archer walking to the center of the compound yard. Walt off to Archer's left, with his rifle covering Jim and James in front of Brenna's house. Herker moving from his post at what was left of the front gates to take his stand to Archer's right. Vernon with his rifle aimed at Brenna's back as she walked toward Matt with bold steps that told him she hadn't asked permission.

"Woman, that's far enough," Vernon warned.

Brenna stopped and brushed the front of her skirt with a decisive pat on her right side as she gave a slight nod over her shoulder toward

Vernon. "Don't worry about me, Matt. I'm prepared to handle whatever, or whoever, comes my way."

Matt smiled outright. Then, for a few seconds, there was no one else, but Brenna. No guns to face. No gold. Just her. His memories traveled back to that day at the creek when an auburn-haired, blue-eyed woman in a yellow blouse dragged him from the water and took him to her home and into her heart. Maybe they'd live through the next few minutes. Maybe they wouldn't. But either way, he'd remember the most beautiful sight he'd ever seen was right here—her blue eyes shining with hope, her auburn braid hanging over her shoulder, and her yellow dress.

"Yellow. Good color for a wedding dress."

"Well, you did request it. A little voice reminded me last night."

Matt nodded. "Thank him next time you talk to him."

"I believe his time here has ended."

"Caddock!"

Matt swung his gaze to Archer.

"I knew you'd come back for her. I'll trade her for the gold. Straight across."

"All right. If that's the way you want it. Parson, dump the gold right here and turn the mules and your horse loose." His intent was to buy John some respect with his preacher standing and to gain him a chance to live to tell the story. "Then get over to the porch and keep your head down." Matt dismounted, pointed Samson toward the barn, and slapped his rump.

Forty feet lay between them for the showdown. Matt welcomed it, craved it. A surge of hot, killing fever coursed through his body then he went icy cold inside. Clear-headed, steely-eyed, fighting mad cold.

Archer pulled his gaze from the bags of gold to gloat at Matt. "Looks like four, maybe five hundred pounds of gold there."

"Closer to six hundred."

Archer's smile widened. "I'll bet it hurts you something fierce to have me take it from you so easy."

Matt took his time removing his leather gloves then tossed them aside all the while watching Archer. "Take it and get the hell out of here."

"I'd like to do that, Matt. I surely would. But I can't have you on my trail the rest of my life. I've got big plans for that gold, and I'm going to enjoy every minute of it." His grin wasn't friendly. "Besides, I promised Vernon he could have your woman after I kill you."

It was meant to rile him, but it didn't work. Vernon was a dead man. He just didn't know it yet.

"Don't count me out just yet. Let's see who really is the better man with a gun, even though we both know the answer to that. You were never a match for me."

Archer laughed. "We had a good run, Matt, but it's over." He spread his feet, elbows out and bent, fingers twitching above the grips of his guns. "I'm gonna take your life and your gold."

Matt opened his duster, flipped the sides behind his holsters, exposing his tied down guns, never breaking the gaze he'd locked on Archer. Around him, the sky took on an eerie gray-green glow. The wintry breeze died to dead calm. The back of his neck prickled from the electricity in the air.

The evening quiet shattered with the booming thunder that came hard on a lightning strike. Matt sensed more than saw Archer go for his guns, but he took out Walt with his first shot before Archer cleared leather. A bullet burned past Matt's shoulder, another went high. A third tugged his coat sleeve. A rapid succession of muffled pops came from his left. From the corner of his eye, he saw Vernon fall face down in the dirt at the same time Herker left the battle from a bullet Matt didn't fire.

Archer walked toward Matt, and Matt met him, firing with each step. He drilled three bullets into Archer's chest, spinning him around. Archer kept his feet, and swung an arm up with a gun bearing down on Matt. Matt felt his leg buckle, and he went to one knee. Archer lumbered toward him, his eyes wild and glassy in his desperation to kill Matt before he died.

Matt helped him along to his reward.

"Matt!" Brenna screamed. "The clouds!"

Billowing, black, churning clouds rolled off McBride Butte. As the maelstrom dipped toward the ground, a herd of red-eyed cattle burst forth as if leaving the bowels of hell in a thunderous race toward the compound with phantom cowboys riding hard to catch them.

Matt staggered to his feet, planting his feet wide to stay upright, while reloading. A keening wail rose on the wind sending cold, shivering dread scuttling down his spine. The riders were coming for him. His time was up. He turned toward them, ready to face his destiny. In the moment, before the herd hit the compound, Brenna screamed his name as she dashed toward him.

"No! Down! Get down!" Matt grabbed Brenna around the waist and took her to the ground, shielding her body with his.

Lightning struck four times in the space of that many heartbeats. Thunder roared and shook air and earth. The acrid stench of Sulphur permeated the air. Expecting it to be the last thing he saw in this life, Matt ducked and cringed as the spectral herd swooped into the compound, their pounding hooves lifting a swirling windstorm of dust as they raced on by him.

Scrambling to her feet, Brenna helped Matt stand, and he leaned on her, accepting her strength as they watched the herd rise high overhead and turn back over the lip of Johnson Mesa to dissolve into the winter storm descending from the west. James and Jim walked up, and Matt noticed the gun in James's hand was the one he'd given to the Parson.

"Matt! Look up there!" Brenna pointed to the clouds.

A cowboy cut out from the ghostriders and fell back from the wild hunt riders. He looked in their direction, tipped his hat, then spurred his horse, and disappeared over the mesa and into the clouds.

"Henry," Matt breathed.

"You released his soul. His debt to the ghost riders is paid, because you kept your promise."

"No. *Promises*. The gold will be put to use the right way, and I found me a good woman."

Brenna rose on her toes and placed a light kiss on his lips. "And I have a good man."

"Just what was that, and what happened here?" James drew his gaze from the sky down to Brenna and Matt. "I'm sure I saw shapes of cattle and men and horses in those clouds. How is that possible?"

Matt managed a tired grin. "It's a story that'll stretch believing."

"Tell me anyway. After experiencing the sight of an empty chair rocking on its own half the night and all the next day, I have amended my willingness to accept the unusual and unexplained."

Matt grunted a chuckle. "Gregory. Well, I'll be damned."

James nodded. "Yes. When Brenna explained why the chair was rocking, Archer and his men spent a rather long, sleepless night holding guns on vacant space."

Brenna interjected, "I took advantage of their superstitious fears with a comment here and there that led them to suspect the chair rocking might be some sort of witchcraft on my part. I gained a great deal of control, which is how I negotiated Jim and Papa's release." Brenna cast a glance toward her house then back at Matt. "I believe it was Gregory's goodbye. The chair didn't stop rocking until Herker yelled out that you were riding in. Gregory's spirt is free now."

"He covered a good many miles since I left here." He smiled at Brenna's quizzical frown. "I'll tell you later."

"What happened to them?" Jim walked a circle, searching the yard. "The bodies are gone. All that's left is the gold."

Matt scanned the grounds. There wasn't a trace of Archer or his men. Gone. Just like Henry.

John shouted, "Rider coming!"

Matt whirled and put himself in front of Brenna with both revolvers clamped in his fists. The sound of a galloping horse neared, then Drew rode through the gate, packing the Winchester like he planned on using it. Jim caught the filly's bridle, and Drew jumped down.

"Matt! Brenna! Did you see that storm? I turned around and came back when I saw the clouds. Billy and his papa went on to Trinidad. Those were the worst clouds I've ever seen. Did you shoot the bad guys? Where are they?" Drew carried on, his attention and curiosity searching the yard for Archer as his questions continued.

Matt gathered Brenna into his arms, burying his face in her hair, and holding onto her for the strength he didn't have right then.

"That was your third time to see the ghostriders."

He nodded. "I guess I changed my ways just in time. If it wasn't for you...for the love you've given a no-account gunfighter, I'd be chasing that devil's herd for all eternity."

Brenna looked at him, smiling through tears. "I do love you, Matt Caddock, despite your guns and the ghostriders and the gold."

"That's good, because you told me to bring a preacher when I returned, and I aim to not disappoint you." He looked past her at John.

A little grin played at her mouth. "I was concerned about what last name to give our child, but now I don't have to worry."

Matt took a step back, his head cocked, eyeing her. "Our child?" A slow grin of understanding spread over his face where confusion had been. "I thought that wasn't possible."

"Apparently, this one is as tough as you are."

Shaking his head, he said, "No. We've got a girl with your feisty spirit and strength."

James asked, "Did I hear correctly that I am going to be a grand-father?"

Brenna nodded. "In the spring."

Matt jerked a nod toward the gold. "Didn't seem right Brenna should marry a drifting gunfighter. Think of it as a reverse dowry. Use it however seems fit."

James rested a hand on Matt's shoulder. "We'll make those decisions as a family."

Snowflakes floated and swirled, and Matt turned his face heavenward. For a few seconds, he closed his eyes to the cool, moist flakes settling softly against his skin. He sent silent thanks on the breeze to Henry and Gregory, wherever their spirits rested now, in well-deserved peace.

Brenna touched his face, and he opened his eyes to her smiling sapphire blue eyes, then he noticed the little gold heart on the chain around her neck. He'd yearned for a home, had hoped he could make one here with Brenna. But until this moment, he'd not given his hopes and heart over completely to those dreams for fear the pain of never seeing them come true would be more than he could stand. Now, that was in his past, just like his gunfighting days. His dreams had come true, and he was going to hold onto them with both hands for the rest of his life—with Brenna.

He unbuckled his gun belt, untied the strings around his thighs, and put the gun belt in Brenna's hands. "Store them with the rest of your guns. I won't need to wear them anymore."

John held out the velvet box, and Matt gave him a grin of thanks as he took it back.

"Gather 'round. The Reverend John Clement's fixing to start a wedding."

About the Author

Native Coloradoan Kaye Spencer grew up on a cattle ranch in northeastern Colorado. Since 1990, she's lived in a small, rural town located in the heart of the infamous Dust Bowl area of the 1930s in southeastern Colorado. Kaye writes mostly western romances.

Louis L'Amour's western novels, Marty Robbins' gunfighter ballads, and western movies and tv shows inspired her love of the American Old West—truths and myths alike. Kaye's favorite movie line is from *Quigley Down Under*: "I said I never had much use for one. Never said I didn't know how to use it." (This is exactly her relationship with her kitchen.)

During Kaye's younger years, she followed the amateur rodeo circuit and experienced life on thoroughbred racetracks. She even did a stint as a cleaner of sugar beet storage silos (after beets are processed into sugar) to keep down the sugar dust in order to minimize static electricity. Otherwise... BOOM! As a single mother, she did manage to find less-explosive jobs to support herself and her three young children.

Having had enough of 'odd' jobs, Kaye entered college to earn a B.A. in teaching. The degree landed her a position as librarian for a 90,000-volume children's library. After that, she returned to college for her M.A. From there, she worked as a teacher of students with special needs, school psychologist, $6^{th} - 12^{th}$ grades English and history teacher, principal, and director of exceptional student services. Some thirty-five years later, she retired. She is fortunate to be able to spend a lot of time with her family. Many rescued and homeless animals have found a home with her, and more are always welcome.

Learn more about Kaye, her books, and where to find her on social media. Her website is www.kayespencer.com

Also by

Chicago Lightning – The Dance
Give Me Tomorrow – Gambling wiht Love